OLIVIA'S

CRY

Chapter One

Ann Baster had been my best friend since first grade, growing up we have been inseparable.

We lived right across the street from each other, I lost my mom when I was very young so Ann's mother became my second mom , when my dad was at work, I was at their house and they treated me like I was their daughter.

We spend every holiday together.

My dad owned three antique stores and on Saturdays Ann and I would hang out with him at the store it was fun to image where the pieces came from and what the people were like that used them so many years ago.

I loved going to the store but as we got older, we found better things to do on our Saturday's.

Like shopping at the mall, or just hanging out with friends.

Ann and I also doubled dated a lot when we got older, which pleased our parents.

They didn't worry so much about us when we were together. We applied at the same college and we were both accepted. I couldn't

Image my life without Ann she had never seemed like just my friend, but she was more like my sister.

So after college when I received a job with an advertising company six hours away from home, it was only natural that Ann moved there with me.

Ann was studying to be a web designer and landed a job just two Doors down from my office.

We rented a two bedroom apartment together.

We had a lot of fun together.

The one thing about Ann and I, we always got along, we told each other everything.

We talked about what we wanted in life ever since we were young girls, and the one thing we both had agreed on was moving out of our town.

We wanted to travel the world, go to places like Paris, and the Caribbean, to Jamaica and the Bahamas, we were going to marry rich men and the four of us would travel together, we would live in luxurious houses.

But then we grew up and faced reality.

When Ann started dating Tony, a colleague of hers,

I knew she was settling for love and not wealth.

Tony was the nicest and sweetest guy I had ever met, and I was so jealous of them.

I wanted to meet someone like Tony, I was also jealous that Ann was moving on with her life without me.

And it wasn't long before our paths would start to drift apart just because She fell in love, I didn't blame her, Tony was a great guy and he had so much going for him and he loved her very much.

Deep down I was happy she had found her soul mate.

I had dated but I hadn't found my prince charming like Ann had.

I was happy for her but I knew I would miss her terribly.

She had a beautiful wedding.

It was the first time my dad had come to visit me and I really enjoyed him staying a few days with me, He also thought of Ann as his other daughter.

Martha and Pete really liked Tony, I knew they missed their daughter the same as I did.

I was lonely when everyone including Ann had left to go back home. I so envied her.

Sometimes I was lonely for my dear friend and I had to learn to do things on my own.

I was happy for Christmas to come around, because that meant I could go home and spend the holidays with my father and Ann and her family.

Ann insisted we drive back home so we could spend more time together

So the three of us left for home three days before Christmas, we had fun on the trip Tony was very funny and he had us both in tears,

I could certainly see why Ann loved him.

They waited until Christmas morning

To Announced they were having twin boys.

They also announced that they were moving to New York.

I was kind of hurt that they hadn't told me on the way here, but I guess they wanted it to be a surprise to me as well.

I could see the shocked look on Martha's face, my heart went out to her, because I knew how much she missed her daughter and now to be away from her grandsons.

Chapter Two

When the day came for Ann and Tony to leave for New York, It was very hard on me.

Tony had been promoted in his job, and it was a good move for them financially it was still hard to see her go. We held each other and cried. It was a sad goodbye.

And then out of the blue my dad called me to tell me he had sold the house that I had grew up in.

He asked me if I could take some time off of work and come home to help him move and sell things in our house.

So I went home to help him get moved into his new house which was farer away from his shop which I couldn't understand but I knew my dad had always had his eye on the older Victorian house.

I can remember every time we drove by it.

He would always say, "One day that will be my house" I just never gave it a lot of thought, until I carried the first box inside, I was shocked.

"Dad why would you want to buy this house, it's so big, why do you need all of this room? It is going to cost you a fortune to heat it."

"I will close off the rooms that I don't use." He said.

I never could understand why my dad did half the things he did, like buying two more antiques shops when he couldn't take care of the one he had, his shop in town needed so much up work done, from the rotten floors to the leaking ceiling, and I knew Dad would never spend the money to pay someone to do the work and the other two shops were also in need of repairing.

I thought instead of buying this big house that he did not need, he could have used that money for the repairs on his shops.

But Dad did what he wanted, and for some reason he wanted this house.

I remember that this old house stood empty for years while I was growing up, it was across town from where we lived but dad often drove by it, he said he was waiting to see a for sale sign up so he could buy it,

I also remembered being glad there never was one. Because I didn't want to move here away from Ann, and besides this big house gave me the creeps.

It was a very pretty Victorian house it had a wide wrap-around porch beautiful railings with cutouts and spindle work. I could see why Dad had always admired this house.

But I still didn't want to live in it, our small two bedroom house was fine for me.

I can't say I was surprised when he told me he had purchased it, Just confused.

I thought it was too big for a single man to live there alone. And when I told him this he would say.

"Ally one day you will raise your family in this house.

But what he didn't know was, I would never move back to this town and certainly not in this house.

My father and I definitely wanted different things in life.

We had a big garage sale and Dad sold almost everything that had been accumulated throughout the years.

He packed papers and pictures in boxes that I'm sure should have gone in the trash.

I wanted to sell my bedroom furniture because I didn't see a need to keep it and move it to the new house, dad wouldn't hear of it, he insisted I set up all my bedroom furniture in one of the bedrooms. So just to please him I did.

It was so sad when everything was moved out because that meant it was our last time in the old house.

That day we had supper with Martha and Pete.

We both cried when we left her home even if the new house was just across town, it still wasn't just across the street.

I knew I would miss it when I came home for a visit and I couldn't run over to Martha's in my PJ's like I had done a thousand times before.

The previous owners had left the house completely furnished with antiques and I'm sure were just as old as the house.

Dad being an antique man, had insisted that everything was to stay where it was. So with Martha's help we cleaned and dusted everything.

After Martha left I was still cleaning in the kitchen when my father came into the room.

"Ally, come here, I want to show you something."

I dried my hands on a towel and followed him to the big porch.

"See that vacant lot next door?"

"Yes" I said as I looked over at it

"That is where your grandparents lived when I was growing up."

"Really, so you lived there as a kid?"

"Yes I did, my mother and father and my older brother your uncle Roy." "I remember Uncle Roy," I said.

My grandparents had passed away when I was four years old so I didn't remember a lot about them.

"Dad why didn't you ever tell me you used to live there when all the times we have passed by here?"

"I just didn't think it was important.

I was sad when it burned down a few years back.

It was like some of my childhood went away. he said I would have liked to known the house you grew up in, I don't even remember what the house looked like because I didn't pay it much mind because I didn't know it used to be your house."

"So Dad is this why you wanted to move here because it was next door to where you grew up?"

"That is one of the reasons." he said, there was a sad tone to his voice.

I was kind of upset with my dad for not telling me this information.

I don't know why he has to be such a private person.

One time I had asked him about my mother and her family. It was like pulling teeth to get some answers.

Then all he told me was that my grandfather moved his family here and that is when he met my mother, he said it was love at first sight, they got married not long after they had met because again my grandfather packed up the family to move away,

They only way my mom could stay here was if the two of them were married.

Dad told me he didn't really get the chance to know my grandparents, so he couldn't tell me much...

When my mother passed away they blamed him.

I had an aunt, dad wasn't sure where she lived, but he gave me her name when I was younger.

I did try to get in touch with her but had no luck because I was should she had married and I didn't have her married name, so after a while I just stop trying.

It had only been me and my dad, but because I grew up with Ann and her parents I considered them my family.

I could tell that dad loved this house, I couldn't understand why until now.

He just had a peaceful look in his eyes as if he was remembering his childhood.

I stayed with Dad for a few days before returning back to my lonely apartment and my Job.

I was glad that Dad was in the house that made him happy, it was big, but as long as he liked it, that's all that mattered.

I could never live there, I didn't like old things.

I didn't care for the old furniture, even though I grew up around antiques and went to many auctions with my father; I still liked the modern look.

Once I was home I started to Miss Ann a lot just thinking about all the things we had shared growing up.

I think that is the reason, when a guy from work asked me out, I accepted, not because I really liked him but because I was lonely.

Steve and I dated for six months, even though I did care for him I knew he wasn't the one for me, our priorities were not the same, I wanted a family and he wanted to party all the time, so I knew I had to stop seeing him and get on with my life.

So when we were alone at work one day,

I told him, "Steve this is just not working with us, we both want different things in life, so I don't think we should see each other anymore."

"Ally, you know I care for you, but I understand what you are saying, I know you want marriage and if I was ready to take that road I would want it to be with you"

He gave me a hug and then walked out of my life as far as dating anymore, we just became friends at work.

It wasn't long before he was dating someone else.

I had often wondered if I had done the right thing.

I didn't know at that time how my life would turn around so drastically.

Chapter Three

Martha called me at work, I was just headed out the door to go home for the day.

"Hey honey" "Hey Martha, It's nice to hear your voice" I said.

"Ally, we are at the hospital with your dad; I think you need to come home."

"What happened? Is he okay?"

"The doctor said he has suffered a heart attack, they are running tests now to find out the severity of the damage, but Ally he is asking for you."

"Tell him I'm on my way." I could hardly see how to pack my bags because of tears that were blurring my vision ,every imaginable thought was running through my mind.

I didn't call my boss until I was seated on the plane.

Once I arrived. I rented a car and drove to the hospital.

He looked so small lying in the hospital bed.

Martha was sitting with him.

She gave me a hug when I walked in.

"So when did this happen?" I asked her

"Yesterday, I stayed with him throughout the day then I went and cleaned his house for you because I knew you would come home, I tried to get him to let me call you when it first happened but you know how stubborn your dad can be, he wanted to wait until test had been done, but today I told him I was calling you, no matter what he says."

Yes I know only too well how stubborn he is." I said.

"He has been sleeping off and on, the Doctor was in just a few minutes ago, before she could say more, Dad opened his eyes and looked at me.

So I walked over to him.

"Hi Dad, how are you feeling?"

"Better now that you are here sweetheart."

"Has the doctor said anything about the test results yet?"

"He said it was nothing too serious.

I can go home in a few days he told me to start eating right, and to start walking.

Alley I need you to move back home and run the store for me."

I knew by him asking me to do this, that he wasn't telling me the whole truth.

"Dad, don't worry about the store right now, you just concentrate on getting better."

"Ally, I'm not saying I'm going to die, but I want you to promise me you will take over the stores for me."

"Of course I will Dad, you know that."

"I didn't want him to stress over his stores so I just agreed but the truth was I hated the thought of moving back and running an antique shop.

I stayed with Dad the rest of the day mostly watching him sleep, and then I went home.

The house was so lonely without dad there, I missed the way things used to be when I was young, I missed my old house I drove by it on the way here and just seeing Ann's house across the street brought tears to my eyes, I missed my friend so very much.

I wasn't comfortable being in this big house by myself, but it did make me feel better to know that Martha had already been here; she had cleaned the house and left a casserole on the stove for me.

Still the house was just creepy for me.

I just didn't understand why my father would want to live in this big drafty house with all of the old furnishings throughout the house.

The only updates were the kitchen appliances.

After I ate, and then a shower I went to bed, I was glad I had the familial feeling of my old bed in this big house.

I had an uneasy sleep; I kept waking up from very strange dreams

I dreamed I was standing at the end of the hallway and at the other end stood a woman, I wasn't scared I was just amazed because she looked like she just walked out of an old movie and she spoke with a southern accent.

She said..."I would never do that to my momma or my daughter."

Then she was gone, I woke up to the smell of baby powder.

I wondered what Martha had used to clean my room with earlier that day but the smell lured me back to sleep.

By morning the dream was forgotten.

I called Martha, to ask her if she wanted to go with me to the hospital, she talked nonstop about her grandsons. "I hate it that Ann lives so far away. My grandsons are not even going to know their grandparents." " Oh sure they will" I tried to encourage her.

"I wish she lived closer to, I miss her so much, but she seems to really like it there. She has made friends with other couples at their church which is good." I said.

Pete and I are going to visit her next month, I'm very excited about that, Oh Ally, It would be wonderful if you could go, and I know Ann would love to see you." Martha said all excited.

"As much as I would love to do that, I wouldn't want to leave dad so soon after his heart attack."

Oh of course what was I thinking, so do you plan on staying here for a while then?"

"I'm staying until I know he is out of danger and back on his feet."

"You are a good daughter." She said as we pulled into the hospital parking lot.

When we arrived to dad's room the Doctor and a nurse was there talking to him giving him some strict rules to follow.

Dad was released after five days in the hospital with diet changes and he was told to walk every day for thirty minutes to start.

Every day was a slow process I made his meals after I threw out all the junk food in the house; thankful the weather was nice, we took walks every day.

I had to promise him I would stay and run the shop, but he had to promise me that he would let me run it and not stress out about anything, and I could tell every day that promise was a challenge for him to keep.

I had been home for two months when I made the decision that I was moving back home for good after witnessing Dad's health declining.

Martha and Pete promised to keep an eye on him while I went back to my apartment, packed my things and got my car, I hated to leave my job, but I knew I needed to be with my dad.

There was a lot to do at the shop but I did manger to talk him into selling the other antique shops he owned and I was very thankful they sold very quickly that was one less thing I had to worry about.

Dad, understood I couldn't manger three shops and still take care of him and the house, I don't know how he did it for all these years and thought maybe that was what caused his heart attack.

Chapter Four

I Had another dream last night, same woman, but the hallway looked so different than it looks now and as I could make out she said the same words "I would never do that to my momma or my daughter" when I woke, I could smell the same scent as before almost like the smell of baby powder, it was so strange.

Did these dreams mean something? I wanted to talk to Dad about it to find out if maybe he had these dreams since he had moved here.

But lately I chose my conversations very carefully around him.

I didn't want to cause him worry.

I could see dad getting thin, I tried to get him to eat, I fixed the things he would ask for, but then he would only take a few bites,

Some days he wouldn't feel like going to the shop with me, it was hard for me to run a business and at the same time worry about my dad at home alone, I found myself getting stressed and the dreams were almost every night now.

The same dream over and over but the other night she added another word she said........

"I would never do that to my parents, Look."

I couldn't understand my dreams, was this woman trying to tell me something, or was I just very over tired from the worry of my job and the health of my father.

One day while at work I had just taken my dad his lunch in the back room where he was resting, many times Ann and I would play house in this little room, but since dad got sick I had the room remodeled into a nice comfortable place for him to rest there was a couch and a big cozy chair, A television for Dad to watch, this way I wouldn't have to leave him home on the days he didn't feel like coming to work with me.

It really helped me having him close.

I was in the front waiting on a customer when we heard a crash in the back room, we both ran to the back to find my dad lying on the floor, the customer started CPR on him while I called 911.

I was shaking so badly and crying it was hard to talk to the operator.

They were there in just minutes.

On the ride to the hospital I knew in my heart my dad was gone.

I was so very thankful for Martha and Pete they helped me with all the funeral arrangements, my father had a trust fund for me as well as a life insurance policy.

Ann came home for the funeral and to be with me and I was so glad because there was nothing I needed more right now then my dear friend.

Chapter Five

The funeral was very nice there were a lot of dad's friends that he had made through the years from having the antique shops they were very kind.

The customer that did CPR on my father went out of his way to be helpful.

That day he stayed with me at the hospital and tried to comfort me until Martha and Pete arrived.

"Jase, thank you so much for what you did for my father and for just being there with me."

"You are very welcome, I wish I could have did more, I felt so bad I couldn't have did more."

"Oh no, you did all you could do, the doctor said dad was dead before he fell to the floor."

"Ally, if you ever need anything, please call me, if you need help at the shop, I know about antiques they are my passion, just call me okay, you have my card."

"Thank you Jase, I might be taking you up on that offer."

After everyone had left the funeral home, Ann insisted she was staying with me for a few days until she went back home to her

Husband and sons, and I didn't argue with her, I didn't want to be alone.

Once we got to my Father's house, I was sure Ann would change her mind about staying.

"Ally surly you are not going to live in this big house?" She said as she looked up at the high ceiling that made the living room appear larger than it truly was.

"No I don't plan on living here" I told her.

"It is pretty I love these old bay windows but I don't care for these heavy drapes, nor this wallpaper but with some work this house could be beautiful, but I still wouldn't want to live here." she said.

"It could be made to be beautiful if you took all of this old furniture out and did some work to it.

But for someone else not me, maybe for someone that enjoys old Victorian houses."

I made coffee and after we were seated

I had decided to tell her about my dreams.

"Ann can I ask you a question?" "Sure" "do you believe that a spirit can come into your dreams to try to tell you something?"

"Do you feel like your dad is trying to tell you something?" She looked worried.

"No, not my dad, ever since I came here to this house I keep having this dream and it's the same dream every time."

"Tell me" she said

"Well upstairs outside of my bedroom door there is a long hallway and I'm standing at one end and at the other end stands a young woman she is dressed the way they dressed a long time ago and in just a whisper she says " I would never do that to my momma or my daughter, look"

And when I wake from the dream the scent of baby powder is in my room."

"Okay that's kind of weird and I just got goosebumps, but no I don't believe in spirits, but what I do believe in, is the fact that for the last year you have been going through so much change in your life, first I leave, and then you break up with Steve and then your dad gets sick.

You not only move back home, but into a strange house and then of course your dad passing away, so what I think is once you sell this place and get your own house, these dreams will stop."

"I hope you are right" I said.

"Do these dreams scare you?" She asked.

"No not at all, they just leave a lot of questions in my mind when I'm up for the day."

"Just dismiss them; hey are you going to sell the antique shop?"

"I don't know yet, I haven't really had time to think about it"

"You are going to need help; do you even know anything about running an antique shop?" she asked.

"Well some but I don't know anything about getting the antiques to the shop or the pricing of them, Jase the guy that was with me when Dad died, you know

I introduced you to him."

"Oh yes the good looking guy." She said with a laugh.

"Anyway" I continued ignoring her remark.

He said he knows all about antiques and said he would help me anytime, so maybe I will ask him to teach me until I can sell the shop, if I decide to sell is, because right now I don't know because I did promise dad I would run it."

"Well you definitely need to talk to this Jase guy."

"I will." I told her.

"It would be so nice if you could sell the house and the shop and come to New York with Tony and me. I would love to have you close by again, I miss you Ally."

"I miss you to , and right now my plans are not to live here, but it will take time to get things squared away before I can go anywhere, I just don't want to go against my father's wishes, but I would hate being here without him" I began to cry again.

"Oh sweetie, I know it's hard right now." Ann put her arms around me.

That's just more reason why you should leave here; there is too many memories here." Ann said and I agreed.

Chapter Six

After going to bed, I tossed and turned, Ann was sleeping in the bed next to me, so I tried to keep still so I wouldn't wake her.

I was standing in the hallway and at the other end, she stood there I noticed how beautiful she was, she was trying to tell me something.

"I would never leave my child, please look!" She said.

"Look at what? What do you want me to look at?" I yelled down the hallway so she could hear me.

"Alley, wake up, Ally, I heard Ann's voice, and I opened my eyes to see Ann's face inches from mine.

"Oh wow, I'm sorry I didn't mean to wake you Ann.

"It's okay, you were having a dream, are you okay?" she asked.

"Ann, can you smell baby powder?" I asked

She sniffed the air a little, yeah a little I can.

Alley, I'm worried about you"

I'm okay, just tired."

"It's no wonder the way you were yelling."

"What did I say?"

"You said "Look at what? "

What did you mean, do you remember?" Ann asked.

"She told me to look, just like she always says."

But I don't know what she wants me to look at?"

"Ally it was just a dream, don't put more into it then just a dream okay." Let's get some sleep."

"I'm sorry I woke you." "It's okay I'm used to waking up with the twins, I miss my boys" she sadly said.

"You will see them in two more days."

"I know and then I will miss you and my parents."

"Why does there have to be miles between us," she said.

"Good night Ally." "Good night Ann."

The next morning we dressed and went to Martha's.

We spend the night there because Martha and Pete insisted, and I didn't want to cause Ann to be away from them, tomorrow she would be going home.

The next day was so very sad; Martha and I cried as Ann boarded the plane, I felt so alone.

I decided to try and open the shop back up and do what I could, I needed something to occupy my mind.

But once there I knew it was going to be hopeless, this place was a mess, Dad had things piled up everywhere, if customers did want to see the things they couldn't,

he had rooms full of antiques that he just put in storage and hadn't got to them yet.

He had so much inventory and yet he kept buying more and more, I definitely had my work cut out for me.

The ceiling was leaking which gave the whole building a musty odor.

I knew if I had not promised my Father, there would already be a for sale on the door tomorrow.

I couldn't handle this mess on my own, that's when I remembered What Jase told me, he said I could call him anytime, so I looked in my purse and took out his business card, it read Jase's Renovation service.

"Hello, may I speak to Jase please"
"Speaking" "Hi Jase, this is Ally"
"Hi Ally, how are you doing?" "I'm doing okay considering everything I guess.
Jase, would you still be interested in helping me out at the shop?"
"Certainly, I can come by in the morning if you would like."
"That would be great, and thank you, I kind of feel lost right now."
"Oh I understand, but don't worry about the shop.
I will help you as long as you need me."
I thanked him and hung up; he gave me a little hope.
I just hoped his service wasn't too expensive.
That night I had another dream, she looked so sad like she wanted so desperately for someone to hear her cry but I didn't understand what she was telling me and in my dream I was trying to understand what she wanted me to look at.

But the dreams never lasted long.

Jase showed up at the shop bright and early with coffee and donuts.

"Good morning Jase, what have you here?"

"Coffee and donuts, hope you like chocolate"

"Oh it's only a girl's passion. Thank you." I said.

"Do you mind if I take a look around?"

"Of course not" as Jase looked around the shop I had my donut and coffee.

"Ally, what are your thoughts here?" "What do you mean?" I asked him.

"I mean are you satisfied with everything?

Or would you like to make some changes here in the shop, I guess I'm asking you, what now?"

"Well the truth is that one day my plans were to sell it, but I made my father a promise, a promise I'm not sure I can keep."

"What would be the reason you would want to sell,

Look at this place, there is so much work that needs to be done it's a mess."

There is a lot of work to be done here, but I see a lot of potential here also.

If it was updated into the twentieth century."

"I don't understand?' I said.

"Your father was very heavy into all antiques, if he liked it, he brought it.

"Yeah, my father was like that with a lot of things," I said.

Your father knew a good bargain when he saw one but his display is lacking attention, Jase continued.

Which is just as important, if the antiques are polished up and displayed right they will sell, but as we both can see here that no one is going to go in a dusty room and rummage through things, but if they were displayed in a more inviting atmosphere it would make all the difference.

This building here is very big so just looking at it, I can already see a profit picture for you."

"I'm listening" I said.

"Okay first you could take these flat tall ceilings and turn them into cathedral ceilings with beautiful function chandeliers that would be a great way to create an eye-catching accent.

Then laminate flooring though out, then you could divide each room into something like you would see in a beautiful Victorian home with furniture, tables and lamps and large rugs on the floor hang pictures on the walls, let the customers feel like they just walked into a cozy living room or a bedroom.

Each room could be different.

Each having different centuries of furnishings, from Modern to contemporary with antiques mixed in with every sitting of the rooms that would make the antiques more appealing.

From lighting and accents, décor and more, this place could go from piled up dusty stuff to an elegant showcase."

The outside storefront could be modernized, because this is a perfect place for this shop being right here on the corner in town and you could have a big sign made that had a catching name."

"How about "LOST TRESURERS" I said becoming more and more interested in what Jase was saying.

"That's sounds great if no other place has that name I like "Lost Treasures"

Just hearing Jase talk about this shop I could almost see what he was saying and I loved what I was visualizing.

"So Jase your card says Renovation services, how long have you been doing that kind of work?"

He laughed. "I've been doing it for about six years now, and also I own and run the Sandcastle B&B on Colfax."

"Oh my goodness, you're the owner of Sandcastle B&B that place is beautiful and I can remember when it wasn't." I laughed.

"Did you do the renovation on it?" "Yes I did, and thank you I'm glad you like it, my sister lives there and does most of the running of it, while I'm at work."

"Wow, I'm impressed." I said.

So how much do you think it would cost to do something like that, if I decide to go that way?"

"If I did it, you would pay for the material and I would do the labor"

"Well that doesn't seem fair to you." I said.

"Well there is a catch" He said with a smile.

"Okay, what is the catch?"

"When I brought the B&B as you know it was in pretty bad shape and had been shut down for many years, well when I opened it up, every room had a lot of very old and expensive antiques in them.

"So I was thinking I could use a room here to sell my antiques, because like I told you antiques are my passion."

And also I could go with you to auctions and get you some good deals.

"Jase, you have a deal. I said.

"Because I don't have a clue about auctions or estate sales or the worth of antiques.

I'm not saying I will continue running this shop, but I'm pretty sure I couldn't get a lot out of it the way it looks right now, so maybe for a year I could run the shop then maybe I can sell it."

"Will you give me first bids on it?" He asked.

"Absolutely" I said with a laugh.

We shook hands on the agreement and I felt good about it.

"Okay so where do we go from here?"

"Well the first thing we do is find out how much you are willing to invest into the renovation, and there would be cost also to the two men that would help me do the work and from there we look at some ideas of what you like."

"Jase, you are the one with the vision and what you have described to me already I love.

So I'm giving you full control on the renovation because after seeing your B&B and remembering what it used to look like, I have full confidence in you and I trust you.

'Okay, when would you like to start?" he said.

"Whenever, you want."

"I will call my crew today and get some plans drawn out."

Chapter Seven

Jase placed the sign on the front door of the shop.

Closed for renovation. And the work began first with the ceilings.

Through the progress of working with Jase it helped to ease the pain of missing my dad and Ann so much, but I did have my moments.

Emptying out the rooms that were not being used with things my father didn't think would sell.

He had a lot of antiques stored away, but with Jase's help we found a lot of beautiful pieces worth a lot of money and then the cramped rooms became beautiful showcase rooms, and I knew a special relationship was also forming between Jase and me.

Even though Jase refused payment for his work I did pay his two men that worked very hard on the project it was well worth it, they did an excellent job.

One afternoon he took me to his B&B to meet his sister and to show me the place.

The Inn was indeed just as beautiful on the inside as the outside.

Jase and his crew did amazing work.

"Carla, this is Ally" Jase said as he introduced us.

"Hi Carla" she looked a lot older than Jase, her appearance reminded me of a librarian, she was very kind and gave me a big hug.

"So you are Ally, I don't think we need an introduction, I feel like I've heard enough about you to know you." She laughed.

"And I'm so sorry to hear about your Dad, he was such a sweet man."

"Thank you, and thank you for the food you sent to my house, everything was delicious, I have been meaning to send thank you cards to everyone, but I've been so busy."

"Oh you are welcome and the people around here don't need thank you cards, we were just so saddened by his passing and were glad to help out."

After a tour of the B&B, Jase went back to the shop and I went home.

"What do you want me to look at? I don't understand what you want me to do?

I awoke in a sweat, and the smell of baby powder.

The smell never lingered long.

I got up and made myself a cup of tea, knowing I wouldn't be able to fall back to sleep anytime soon.

I went over the dream trying to put anything together if indeed there was anything to place together but I was convinced this was not just a dream.

"What was she trying to tell me? " I would never do that to my parents, please look."

If I only knew what she wanted me to look at?

The next morning, I had a headache and I knew it was because of lack of sleep, I couldn't wait to sell this old house.

I had a lot of work to do at the shop today getting things out of the next room, and the last I looked the room was packed, so today I wasn't looking forward to tackling it with this headache.

I was happy to see Jase had already begun, glad I had given him a key to the shop, because they started their work very early

"Oh thank you Jase, sorry I'm late, but I had a hard night."

"No problem, there is a lot of furniture and things in this room, we have a lot of good things to go into our finished rooms, everything needs a good cleaning."

"Jase, I love all of the ceiling lights. They make this whole place looked warm and inviting, how can I ever repay you for all the hard work you have done?"

"You can out with me?"

What? Seriously?" I not only sounded shocked I was acting shocked.

"Yes I'm serious." "Okay, I will go out with you" I laughed.

"I will pick you up at seven O'clock."

"Okay." I said.

The rest of the day felt kind of strange just knowing I had a date with Jase.

I liked Jase a lot, but I just figured he seen me as just a casual business associate and nothing more.

After the room was empty the guys started tearing up the floors and replacing it with beautiful hardwood.

While they were doing that, we started on the last room.

Tomorrow, we would start placing the appropriate furniture in the rooms after cleaning each item.

I went home and took a long bath and got ready for my date with Jase.

Jase was so charming, we went to dinner and then to a live comedy show, we laughed so hard, I couldn't ever remember having such a good time before.

When Jase walked me to my door, he kissed me good night.

Kisses that I let linger on my lips.

As I lay in bed I thought about our date and I drifted into a sweet sleep.

When I got to the shop the next morning Jase was not there which was strange, his guys were painting the last room.

I started to clean the furniture, I knew after all the rooms were done and the shop was ready to open, Jase would have no need to come here every day, and I already missed him just thinking about it.

Just as I was hanging the last picture in one of the rooms Jase came in the room.

"Oh wow, this is beautiful" he said.

"I know. I could live here, thanks to you and the guys."

"And thanks to you, you have a knack for decorating."

"We make a good team" The words were out of my mouth before I could stop them, I could feel the heat coming from my face.

He walked over and took me into his arms. "We make a great team."

Chapter Eight

When the guys had the last room ready for us; we started placing the beautiful colonial bedroom suit that my father had stuffed in a back room into the new finished room.

I took all the drawers out of the dresser and chest to clean everything when I took the two drawers out of the vanity I noticed a small piece of wire sticking out and when I pulled on it a small drawer opened and inside was a diary, I held the book in my hands it had a single pink faded rose at the top, the pages were yellow from age

I carefully opened the front page it read Olivia's thought book

"Jase, can you come here for a minute please"

"Yeah," he said as he walked into the room wiping his hands on a rag "Look at what I found in a secret drawer" I held the diary up to him. He took it and looked at it. "Wow, this is very old."

" I know, look at the drawer it was in, what a great hiding place"

"How did you discover that?" I showed him the little wire hanging down, then I pulled it to show him the drawer." " Pretty neat huh?"

He laughed. "I would say so."

After the room was all set up I placed a beautiful embroidered old Victorian bedspread on the bed,

I had found in the closet of my house after cleaning it, I brought to the shop.

Along with the pillows, it was beautiful. I can't believe my father had this hid away.

"So after tomorrow, I think we are ready to open."

"Really, you think so?" "Why not, it won't take us long to set the other two rooms up as soon as things are delivered tomorrow."

"But shouldn't we advertise the opening?"

"Yes of course, I'm just getting ahead of myself, can you do that?"

"Yes, I can, I worked in advertising, remember?"

"Okay then you can take care of that and I will take care of the grand opening."

"Okay, good night Jase, see you in the morning..."

"Good night Ally."

After my shower, I took the diary out of my bag and started to read.

Chapter Nine

March 2nd 1906

Matthew came by today, wanted to know if I cared to take a walk with him, I knew momma and poppa would be very disappointed if I didn't go, so I went with him, I didn't know Matthew that well, he was older than James and me, even though we lived next door to each other it was James that I played with when we were kids.

And hung out with when we got older, Matthew was always with the older boys, and he was never at home.

Matthew was always mean to James and me when he was around.

We walked in the flower garden and then down the pathway toward the towers it was a beautiful walk and the conversation was good we talked of casual things, and in my mind I thought Matthew would be a good brother-n-law.

But I knew his Intensions were to marry me.

How could he not know I was in love with his brother James?

James and I grew up together, we had always remained friends and we both knew one day, we would marry, but our families had other plans.

When they discovered James and I were falling in love, and we wanted to get married they separated us and we weren't allowed to see each other anymore.

My parents always thought of James as trouble, because one year he started hanging around with a bad crowd and had got caught stealing.

But after he got caught, he stopped hanging with them and he was good, but they didn't care because what was done was done in their eyes. Even his own family treated him like the black sheep of the family just because he made one mistake.

But they didn't know James like I did.

James and I wanted to get married, but his parents said it was out of the question.

Both of the families had already decided a long time ago that I would marry Matthew.

I wasn't aware that this was what our families had in their minds and I would never in a million years marry Matthew and I'm sure he felt the same way, Matthew didn't even like me.

But James didn't bother telling me, he just broke up with me and broke my heart.

He started running around with a wild gang and got into trouble with the police.

I didn't find out about their plans about Matthew and me until James got coughed and brought back home to face the music.

He came to my house the day he returned home, I heard Poppa tell him, he could no longer see me.

Late that night he came to my window and we talked and that was when he told me the agreement our parents had, and they were going to make me marry Matthew. He told me he loved me still and I believed him.

That is when we found our secret hiding place and we met there every other afternoon.

March 8th

I went with poppa to Atlanta, we were gone for five long days, and I didn't like the trip because Poppa kept telling me all the good qualities that Matthew had.

"Poppa, is it true that you and Momma want me to marry Matthew?"

"Daughter, we feel like it would be very good for you to wed Matthew,

He will make a good husband and he is a good provider.

"But Poppa, I don't love Matthew, I love James."

"Olivia, you can just forget about James, I will never let you marry that boy."

I didn't say anymore, I knew when my Poppa had made up his mind, there was no changing it."

I just held in my tears.

I was glad when the trip was over and I was back home.

I miss you James, I can't to see you.

March 9th

I overhead momma and Poppa talking after breakfast this morning, they talked about my upcoming wedding; they said it would take place in two weeks.

How could they sleep at night knowing how sad I was to marry Matthew?

I thought Parents wanted their children to be happy.

I feel like right now they only care about getting me married off and out of their house.

My parents and I have always been so close and I have never gone against them in any decision they have had for me, but this is almost out of the question.

Oh James I wish I could talk to you; to see you I need you my love.

March 11th

Today I finally got up the nerve to talk again too my parents about Matthew, it didn't go so well, it was like their minds were closed to how I felt.

I tried to explain to them that I was not in love with Matthew and that it was James I loved, and James I wanted to marry.

As I listened to their explanations on why I should marry Matthew, I reasoned in my mind what I was going to do, I was going to find James and run away with him, I didn't want to go against my parents, I loved them very much but I also Loved James very much, and I didn't feel like Momma and poppa were taking my best interest or my happiness into consideration so I felt like I had no other choice but to run away with James, or spend the rest of my life in misery.

Momma said one day I would understand the reason that it was good that I marry Matthew.

I asked them why Matthew?

Because he is stable and has his own business and he is the Eldest son and he would provide for his family.

All I heard was a lot of and's but not anything about love or happiness.

Oh James two more days until I see you, I miss you my darling.

Chapter Ten

I Jumped when my phone rung.

"Hello" "Hey Girl, what are you up to?" "Hi Ann, not much, just reading a book"

I didn't want to get into what I had found and that I was reading Olivia's diary.

"So did you go out with Jase again yet?"

"How is Jase, any wedding plans yet? " Ann I just talked to you two days ago and no there are no wedding plans nor was there a proposal. But if and when there is, I promise you will be the first to know."

I think I made a mistake telling Ann about my date with Jase, now she would forever tease me about it.

"How are my nephews doing?" I asked

"They are awesome and driving me a little crazy" she laughed.

"Ally, you told me the dreams have stopped, is that still the case?"

"The last dream I had was two days ago, so as of now no dreams."

"I was just thinking about the dreams today so I thought I would ask you, I'm glad they have stopped I could tell they had you worried."

"Oh I'm fine, Guess what, the shop might open by the weekend, it is so pretty I wish you could see it, it is nothing like it used to be."

"I'm happy for you Ally, I will visit soon, you know for the wedding," she laughed.

When I hung up the phone, I put the diary away.

I had an ad to work on for my shop's grand opening.

"Tell me what you want me to look at, I don't understand, I cried.

"If you look, you will find that I could never do that to my parents."

I woke to the smell of the baby powder again.

I tossed and turned until I finally fell back to sleep.

The next morning I dropped my ad off at the newspaper, then I went to the library to print off flyers and also I hung up a poster announcing our opening.

Then I went to the B&B to give Carla a poster to hang at the inn.

When I got to the shop Jase had just finished placing the modern furniture in the rooms, it was beautiful.

"Jase it's so pretty, everything is just like you said it would look. Thank you."

"Can't you show your gratitude with a kiss?"

So I walked over to him and I gave him a kiss.

"By the way, Martha called for you." He said.

"Oh okay, I will call her back, the ad has been dropped off at the newspaper and I put a poster at the library and at your inn.

I handed him the flyers.'

"These are amazing, good Job."

"Thank you, I said as I walked over to the phone to call Martha.

Martha wanted to know when we were opening.

She and Pete were going to sit up a table with homemade cookies and coffee.

"That is so sweet of you, thank you so much. We will open Saturday.

After the shop was spic and span and everything was in place, Jase took me to dinner.

I was anxious to get home and relax and read the diary, it had been on my mind all day, and I felt like I was stepping back in time when I was reading it.

I took a long hot bath trying to relax. I couldn't seem to get Oliva out of my mind, I wondered about her, what she looked like, where she lived with her family, was the bedroom suit hers?

Knowing it almost had to be hers since that was where her diary was at, I wondered if she had forgotten about it being there.

I got out of the bath and after dressing into my pajamas I took a blanket and sat on the couch with the diary.

I almost felt like I was invading Olivia's privacy by reading her diary but I was driven to find out if she would marry Matthew or James?

March 14th

Knowing that Poppa had forbidden me to ever see James again, I sneaked down the winding old brick staircase holding my flashlight close. I walked slowly as not to trip…

It felt so good to be in James's arms, I wanted to stay there forever.

I keep going over the conversation we had last night.

"James they are going to make me marry Matthew, what are we going to do?"

"Olivia, run away with me, we can leave in the morning before it is light outside, it's the only way."

My mind was made up to ask James to run away with me but when he said the words, I knew I could never do that to my parents

James was very sad when I refused.

"But Olivia there is no other way, my parents are very determined that you and my brother will marry."

I love you with all of my heart and It's me you should be marrying not Matthew."

"James can't you talk to your parents and make them see, that this is wrong. That we love each other and want to get married."

"Don't you think I have tried, they won't hear of it "But why does Matthew want to marry me, there are a lot of girls that he could marry."

"But I'm not in love with another girl, I'm in love with you and he can't stand that, Matthew has always wanted what he can't have.

My parents are very old fashion they think the oldest son should marry first.

It was an agreement between your parents and mine, that you would marry Matthew went the time was right.

"But that is not fair, I'm not marrying Matthew, I don't love him, I love you James I cried.

He held me.

"Olivia that is why running away is our only chance to be together."

"But it would break my parent's heart if I left
I just don't think I can do that them, and then what if something happened to them, I would never forgive myself.
I have to have time to think about this, there has got to be another way,
I will stand up to them and tell them I will not marry Matthew.
I heard a notice.
"James. I have to go, meet me here Thursday night."
I walked way fast; I got really frightened for some reason like we were being watched and I didn't wait for James's answer.

Chapter Eleven

I dropped the book to my lap, Was Olivia the girl in my dreams? Was it her that was trying to tell me something?

Now I knew my dreams had nothing to do with this house but I think it does have something with that bedroom suite and the vanity I found this diary in.

I broke out in a cold sweat, Okay this is just crazy I told myself.

It's just coincidental she spoke almost the same words as in my dreams.

I knew I needed a break from this, so no more reading tonight.

I needed to get back to my century and forget this for now.

I was letting my imagination run wild.

I fixed myself a snack and tried to think of something else.

Looking around at this big house, I wondered what it looked like when it was first build, I could image it was beautiful.

I wondered if there were children that grew up here.

For some reason I couldn't see children here, this house held a depressed feeling, like no joy had ever been here, but I know children could have brought this big house to life.

But there must have been children because there are five very small bedrooms upstairs and one bedroom downstairs.

That is the bedroom my father used.

His things were still in that bedroom, I just never have gotten around to packing his things up

I missed my dad, I had no other family members that I knew of, I had an aunt but I couldn't find her.

My Dad had one brother that had passed away when I was a young girl, I was truly all alone in this world besides my dear Friend and her family, they were the only Family I really only knew.

As much as I knew I should just stop reading this young girl's personal thoughts, I picked it back up and opened the pages again.

March 21st

It has been a week since I have seen James.

My heart is so heavy,

I couldn't get away last Thursday, because Matthew decided to come to our home to talk to Poppa.

I didn't like it when Momma asked him to stay for supper.

I also didn't like the way he looked at me.

I felt like I was on an auction block.

He was always very kind when he was around my parents, but I knew him long enough to know that was just an act.

Growing up and being at his house, he was anything but kind. He was a bully to me and James.

I know James was there waiting for me.

I wish I had a way to get word to him to meet me tomorrow.

I knew I would just have to take a chance and go there, in hopes he would be taking the same chance.

March 25th

Matthew will come tonight for me I overheard him telling Poppa he wanted to escort me to the dance, I did not want to go with him.

But I felt I had no choice, when momma told me to dress nice and that Matthew was coming for me, I took this chance to talk to her.

"Momma, I don't love Matthew, please don't ask me to marry him."

"Olivia, I understand right now you don't love Matthew, but one day you will, trust your father and me."

"How do you know I will ever love him?"

"When I was your age, your grandmother and Grandfather forced me into marrying your father and I did not love him, I didn't even like him, but in time we got to know each other than we had you ~~and you~~ my dear. You brought not only joy into our lives but you brought love.

Your father became my best friend,"

How long did it take you to fall in love with Poppa?"

"Oh Olivia, as long as two people get along together love is not important."

"Momma, have you ever been in love with poppa?'

"I love your poppa, yes" she turned away from me, as if she couldn't look me in my eyes.

"But you are not in love with him." I asked her.

I felt so sad for her.

As we walked Matthew reached out and took my hand, I almost froze.

"Matthew, can I ask you a question?"

"It depends on the question."

'Have you always known that our parents wanted us to marry?" " I have known for a while."

"Matthew, you have never acted like you even liked me, so why now? Do you want to marry me?"

"What do you mean I have never liked you? I have always liked you."

"Then why were you so mean to me, growing up?"

"Maybe I was mean to you because you were with my little brother, when you should have been with me."

"But Matthew, you knew James and I have always talked about getting married, you also know that we love each other, so why would you want to marry me, knowing that?"

"Olivia, maybe you think that you loved my brother, but I know for a fact James does not love you."

"I can provide a good home for you, but James will only cause you heartache and he will hurt you. You will get over James in time and who knows maybe one day you will feel about me the way you feel about him."

"Matthew I'm sorry, I'm not trying to be mean but I love James and I always will."

"That is just a chance I'm willing to take."

We didn't speak about it anymore because I knew Matthew was not going to listen to reason. His mind was set just like my parents.

I prayed the night would end soon... When Matthew took me in his arms for the dance it was all I could do to stop myself from running away from him.

At the end of the night when he walked me to my door he said.

"You do know Olivia that we will wed soon."

"Matthew you don't love me."

"I don't believe in love," He said.

When he walked me to my door, he tried to kiss me good night, but I pulled away from him and ran into the house, I heard him laugh.

I believed now that Matthew was in love with me but I knew I would never return that love.

My heart was already taken.

March 23rd

Momma came into my room today to talk to me about my wedding dress, I told her I didn't care what dress I wore or what it looked like, my heart was not in this wedding or this marriage.

I told her if her and Poppa made me go through with this; they were condemning me to a life of sadness. She told me they were doing it out of love and one day I would understand that, she also told me I was being very dramatic.

I knew I had to talk to James somehow.

He was right running away was the only answer so that is what I had to do, One day after James and I are married I will return and ask for their forgiveness for going against them,

When I was sure Momma and Poppa were sleeping, I wrote them a note and I packed my clothes, I was so sad to think I wouldn't see my parents again for a long time. Tomorrow I would find James and tell him I will go away with him.

March 24th

I hoped no one saw me going to our secret hiding place, Oh James where are you? I sat on the steps and cried, I knew he had no idea I was here waiting for him.

"Why the tears," I heard someone say. I jumped to my feet.

"It was Matthew and James's sister. What are you doing here?" No one knew about this place how did she find it?

"My little brother said you would be here waiting for him, he told me to give you a message." "Where is he, why didn't he come here?" I asked.

"Little brother left town with Abigail.

"That is not true." "Yes Olivia, it is true, they are to be married, and he wanted me to tell you he is very sorry, but he couldn't deny his feelings any longer."

"I don't believe you; Matthew put you up to this, didn't he?"

"Olivia, you can stay here and wait for James as long as you want but he won't come." She walked away.

I ran home and went straight to my room.

I laid on my bed and cried, was what she told me true, would James really do this to me, I know as kids there was a short time that he liked Abigail, but we were just kids then. I know James loves me.

Was it because I wouldn't run away with him, I can't believe the way my life is turning out.

I knew in my heart that James would never just leave me and go away with someone else, because he could had did that at any time, I know he loves me.

I have known all my life that James was the only one for me, he was my best friend, the one that knew all of my secrets he has always been there for me, and he has never let me down before.

I couldn't believe what his sister told me, I know somehow Matthew has something to do with this lie.

He has always acted like he hated James...

I think it was because he was jealous of his younger brother and he has always wanted what James had.

And I believe that was the only reason Matthew wanted to marry me is because he knows how much James loves me, and he is going to make sure that James and I never get married.

I will not marry Matthew. I will not lose the only man I love to marry the man that I do not love.

I have to find a way out of this marriage.

I had to find a way to talk to James.

Growing up around his family, his parents were always nice to me until I get older, then they didn't want me coming around anymore.

And James was forbidden to see me.

So James and I had to meet in our secret place.

How did his sister know of it unless James had told her?

March 15th

Momma and poppa called me into the sitting room to talk to me, which was good, because I needed to talk to them also.

"Olivia, it is true that James ran off with Abigale

I had a talk with her father and he confirmed it

We have told you before that James is trouble and this proves it.

Your mother and I are getting older and we want to see your settled down with a responsible man, and we both feel like Matthew is that man, we would like to see grandchildren before we pass on, so please don't take that from us.

I started to cry because of the hurt James has put on me,

I didn't believe he could be with Abigale and it hurt me so much just to picture them together, every word that James has told me was a lie, I could never forgive him, but I still could never stop loving him and I hated that for me.

I told my parents I would marry Matthew and I walked out of the room.

Nothing really even mattered to me anymore, I was so hurt.

I know for some reason the wedding had been postponed and I hoped they had come to their senses and seen that this was a bad idea.

That they knew they were hurting me by making me marry someone I didn't love. I couldn't understand my parents when their parents made them get married so they knew how I felt.

That should have been reason enough not to force me into it.

I hadn't heard from James so I knew it must be true, he ran away with Abigale and he had been lying to me all this time and I have been a fool.

April 16th

Momma helped me get dressed, as she was placing the vail on my head; she said again that one day I would understand why I should marry Matthew.

"Olivia, I know you think you have feelings for James but honey, it is not love its friendship, and you just can't tell the difference right now because you have lost that friendship and you are hurt.

I wanted to say to her that she knew nothing about being in love, and she shouldn't be talking to me about something she knows nothing about.

But I held my tongue.

How could James have loved you and then run away with another girl?"

"I told her that the friendship part didn't make any sense

"Momma I do love James and I always will, no matter if I'm married to Matthew or not.

Even if he has ran off with someone?"

Olivia, your father felt the need to tell you after Matthew told your father and me that his brother had run away with that girl.

Matthew didn't want to tell you because he knows how close you two are, and he didn't want to spoil your special day."

"Momma this is not my special day, this is the most horrible day of my life" I ran into the other room and closed the door behind me...

I stayed there until my father knocked on the door.

Then he led me to a room where I was soon to walk down the aisle and marry Matthew,

I hated to make momma feel bad today, but why should I care about her feelings when her or poppa didn't care about my happiness.

I would never go against my parents, but I didn't agree with them.

When it was time for Poppa to take my hand to lead me down the aisle to marry Matthew I cried.

I knew they thought they were doing what was best for me in the long run and I know they prayed one day I would grow to love Matthew and be happy.

They looked at James as a trouble maker and they thought he would never change or grow up to be the man his brother was, but James wasn't like that anymore, he has grew up and he loved me, I just know he does.

Did James love Abigail?

The girl we would run away from when we were kids.

Did they now run away from me?

I know Matthew and everyone attending the ceremony today mistook my tears for happiness.

I knew the day would never come that I would forget James

And I knew I would never fall in love with Matthew.

But I did hope the day would come that I would find it in my heart to forgive Momma and Poppa

For ruining my life and making me spend the rest of it with a man I didn't love.

Chapter Twelve

I Placed the diary back into my nightstand drawer, I felt a saddest, and I couldn't believe she married Matthew.

Again I thought about Jase, I knew I was in love with him and sometimes he acted the same toward me, I couldn't even picture myself with anyone other than Jase, that I have never declared my love to like Olivia and James has done.

So I can't even image this poor girl who had to marry a man she did not love and to lose the one man she did love.

Children were sure loyal to their parents back in those days.

I couldn't understand how Olivia's parents could do that to their daughter.

I wondered again if it was possible that my dreams had anything to do with this diary or was I just being paranoid?

I decided to go to bed early tonight because tomorrow was a big day and I hoped I wouldn't dream tonight I needed rest for tomorrow.

Again I woke up to the same confusing smell.

But this dream was different. I didn't want to forget what she said.

I took a pad and pen out of the nightstand drawer and wrote it down.

"Please know I would never do that to my little girl or my momma because of our love I lost. Look and you will find."

Oh my goodness I wish I knew what I was supposed to look for?

Did Olivia have a child with James?

Now I knew for a fact this was not just a dream.

This young lady wanted me to find out something but what?

I still felt like the answer had something to do with the furniture.

Did it belong to Olivia's parents?

I had so many questions.

I wondered if I could find out who owned it back then, maybe I would find an answer to why I was having these dreams and what she wanted me to look at?

Everything was all set up for our grand opening; I really hoped neither of us would be disappointed today we had did so much work the last few weeks and I prayed it paid off.

Martha and Pete had the table sit up very nice with coffee and treats.

We had balloons hung everywhere that read grand opening.

Jase gave me a kiss for luck, and then he unlocked the door.

By mid- morning the shop had quite a few people looking around, we even made some good sales.

I was standing with Jase behind the counter having a cup of coffee when

He pointed out to me a man talking to Carla,

"See that guy, he stays a lot at the Inn, I really think he likes my sister, but they are both so shy they haven't been on a date yet."

"Well do you think Carla likes him?" I asked.

"Are you kidding she is crazy about him, that's all she talks about is Joe"

"Jase, we should help them out by going on a double date with them"

"Man, Ally you will do anything to go out with me again." He laughed.

"Whatever!" Just then a potential buyer came up to us.

At the end of the day I was exhausted but very happy with the day's results.

After thanking everyone who helped us, Jase and I were alone...

"Well this was a pretty good day huh?"

"Yes this was a wonderful day, Thanks to you,"

"Hey thanks to you also, and most of all." He said...

"Jase if I hadn't met you, I would still be feeling so lost about my father's store and his wishes, you have no idea how you helped me find myself and if it weren't for you I would still be standing in a not up to date junk filled dusty big building with no hope, but now look at it, it is beautiful and elegant and I love it.

I want to stay here instead of going home, because my house minus all the junk and dust is in the same shape this shop used to be and I hate it."

"Then change it." Jase said.

"I'm going to; I'm going to sell it."

"If you change your mind, I know of a good contractor I would highly recommend for the job and I'm pretty sure that "Lost treasures".

On the corner would give him a good recommendation, just ask for the beautiful owner of the shop, her name is Ally and I am madly in love with her."

I know my eyes got as big as saucers with his last statement.

"You are?" "Come on Ally, you have to know that.

Do you really think I would have did all of this work for free for anyone else?"

"But I thought it was for exchange for you to display your antiques here."

"Really? How much money do you think I have in a few pieces of antiques?

I could have put anywhere?" We both laughed.

"Okay I did think that was odd, but I didn't want to mention it."

"Oh Jase, I love you to, but I was so scared, I wouldn't let myself think about it."

"I was kind of scared to let you know how I felt because Of the rejection I may have got from you, but I'm so very glad you love me to." He smiled...

He took me in his arms and kissed me.

"My sister is going to be very happy."

Why is that?" I asked. "Because from the beginning she told me I was in love with you, and she was right."

After we locked up, Jase walked me to my car and said good night.

I went home, showered, and went to bed, I thought about Jase and about how happy he made me, I couldn't wait to call Ann tomorrow.

I was excited to see Jase the next morning, because now it was different.

He didn't stay at the shop long, he had other work to do now, and I missed him.

Business was good and I thought about hiring someone to help me.

Chapter Thirteen

At Lunch Martha came down and brought me a sandwich.

"What a pleasant surprise, I wasn't expecting you here today."

I gave her a hug.

"I know, but there is a picture here I saw it yesterday and I have decided I wanted it."

We talked for a while and I told her, I was thinking about hiring someone for part time here.

"That would be great, you can hire me." "You, I didn't know you were looking for a job?" I said.

"Oh Ally, I'm so bored with Pete working all day and Ann and the boys living so far away I have nothing to do, working here part time would be a prayer answered for me."

"Okay, you are hired, you can start tomorrow." "Wonderful, okay I'm going get my picture and head home."

Martha purchased a beautiful antique picture that was hanging in one of the rooms.

Jase called me just before I closed the shop for the day.

"Hi, I was hoping to get done in time to stop by be to see you before you went home, but we ran into some problems so I didn't make it but I wanted to call and say good night and to tell you I love you."

"Thank you, that was very nice of you, I love you too, Good night Jase."

After I ate, and in my pajamas I called Ann.

"Hey girl, I have some news." "About your grand opening, Mother said it went great." "Yes it did, we had a great day, but that wasn't my news."

"Oh sorry, tell me." she said.

"Jase told me he was in love with me yesterday." I know she heard the excitement in my voice.

"Oh Wow! That is good news, so what did you say?'

"I told him I loved him, of course."

"Ally, I'm so happy for you, it looks like your life is coming together." "I know it is, and I am so very happy.

"Well you deserve to be happy." she said.

Now I just got too put this house on the market, and find me a house closer to the shop."

"Okay, promise me you will call me and keep me updated on you and your new found love" she teased.

"I promise, have a good night."

Once I was in bed, I carefully took the diary out of the drawer and opened up the pages.

June 17th

I haven't felt like writing for the last few months
I haven't really felt like doing much of anything.
Matthew said maybe after supper tonight, we could go visit Momma and Poppa, the last time I seen them was last week when they came here, they both looked depressed and the only thing I could think of was they deserved it, I think now just after only a few weeks, they were getting to know the real controlling Matthew.
But it was a little too late, I did what my parents insisted on me doing, because I wanted to be a good daughter, and now we all will pay the price, they can be unhappy with me.
When they were here last week, there wasn't a lot of talking between them and Matthew.
I could tell they were very uneasy being here.
And they cut their visit short.

June 18th

But we didn't go to my parents and I wasn't surprised, I'm finding out very quickly that he is not a man of his word, while we were having our supper Matthew sad he was too tired to go visit my parents tonight, so I asked him if it would be okay, if I went to visit them for a little while he said no.

"Matthew, I have been waiting all day to see Momma and Poppa, I won't be gone long I promise" I reached for my coat.

He got to his feet and stood in from of face very closely and said.

"Tomorrow we can go but not tonight" he took my coat out of my hand.

Now clean the dishes, then he walked into the other room.

June 19th

Matthew brought me flowers this evening when he came home from work, I knew he was trying to make up from yesterday, he knew I wanted to see my parents, but he said he was too tired and it was out of the question that I go alone, I think he was scared I wouldn't come back.
But getting flowers from Matthew meant nothing to me.
The only thing I wanted from him was my freedom.
I realize now that the only person to blame for my unhappiness was myself, I shouldn't have given in but I should have fought and stood my ground and I should have never married Matthew.

June 21

As I was fixing Matthew's breakfast before he went to work

He told me I could invite my parents here for supper tomorrow evening.

I thanked him.

That made me very happy it was hard to stay away from them when they only lived two houses down from me.

It got so lonely here all day alone and I knew Momma wouldn't come to visit unless she was invited.

After Matthew left for work, I got dressed and went to momma's

She acted like she was very happy to see me I stayed for a while after I had invited them to supper it felt so nice to be back home

I didn't want to stay to long just in case Matthew came back home for some reason.

June 23th

Momma and Poppa came for supper last night. I made pot roast because I knew it was Poppa's favorite.

We had a nice visit, Matthew was very pleasant, and the whole evening was joyful, I was sorry to see it end.

After the kitchen was all cleaned up I was getting ready for bed.

"Do you still love him?" "What?" I turned around to see Matthew standing in the door way. "Do you still love James?"

"Matthew, I'm married to you now. I don't feel comfortable when you asked me questions like that.'

I continued to get ready for bed. He came over and swung me around to face him. "I asked you a question and you will answer me, do you still love my brother?"

"No! Matthew." I jerked away from him, I knew I had to say no, because the last time he asked which was two days after our wedding, I said yes and he hit me, and I didn't want that again, so it was just easier to say no.

If he only knew that James was on my mind every minute of the day.

Why did James leave me, why didn't he fight for me, was it because he really didn't love me?

Maybe he did love Abigail.

I wondered if he knew that Matthew and I got married, or if he even cared.

With those thoughts the tears came, I was glad it was dark and Matthew couldn't see me cry.

I knew somehow I needed to forget James It wasn't right to be married to Matthew and being thinking of his brother, I just didn't know how to stop loving James, but I wanted to.

June 27th

I Think I'm pregnant, I pray I'm not because as much as I want a child, I don't want to bring a baby into this marriage and this unhappiness.
It was meant for James to be the father of my children.
We have talked about it so many times, we wanted a boy and a girl, we even had our names picked out for them, we had made so many plans through the years, we would sit in his back yard on a bench and talk about our wedding, our family we were going to have, I thought we were so in love.
All of my plans along with my dreams are gone just like my love. Gone
I had big dreams, but now I was living my nightmare.

Chapter Fourteen

July 11th

I went and spend the day with Momma yesterday while Matthew was at work, it felt good to be alone with her and just to be able to talk to someone I missed her.

I told her of my suspicion, she was over joyed, and I wondered how Matthew was going to feel about having a baby.

Would he be mad? Would he accuse me of being unfaithful to him? And believe the baby belong to James?

I never knew what was in Matthew's mind from one day to the next.

But I just couldn't believe it would be a happy occasion for him, because nothing was.

But for once I was glad James was gone because he couldn't accuse me.

July 23th

I have little time to write now days, with the taking care of the home and having Matthew's supper on time, he is very picky about his meals, tonight Matthew's parents and his sister will come for supper tonight the house is cleaned and I have everything under control, but I'm still nervous, I do hope there is news about James, and if there is I must act unconcerned, I know it's wrong but I think about him every day and I wonder if he married Abigail?

I wondered if he was happy

I already knew Matthew's parents didn't like me and the truth was I didn't care much for them, I just wanted this meal to be done, and they could leave.

Matthew acted like he was scared of them and I can't really blame him, they can be very mean at times.

July 24th

Supper went well last night, I didn't much care how all three of them gave me dirty looks, everyone at the supper table knew that I was in love with James and I felt so uncomfortable and I was very glad when they went home, I could get my fighting over, with Matthew and then go to bed.

Because I could tell by the way he kept giving me dirty looks during our meal, I wasn't doing something right.

I tried to talk to his mother, but she was very shape with me so I didn't talk I just sat there while the conversation was going on.

I wanted so much to go into the kitchen and start to clean the dishes, but I didn't want to be rude, or listen to Matthew after they went home.

They seemed to stay a long time after the meal was over.

I was so happy to hear his father say, they should be going.

After they left, I started to clear the table.

"Leave that until morning I'm going to bed and I don't want to hear you in here banging the dishes around.

I wasn't sleepy so I sat in the big chair to read a book, something I never seem to have time to do. I had on a very dim light as not to disturbed Matthew.

After only a few pages, Matthew came into the room and knocked the book out of my hand.

"What do you think you are doing? He demanded.

"I'm not tired so I was going to read for just a little while" I said.

"I told you I was going to bed, and that means lights out.

He turned and walked back into the bedroom after he tuned the light off.

August 10th

Today I have decided to tell Matthew I was having a baby because I knew I was almost four months and I couldn't hide it any longer.

I hoped he would be happy,

Maybe it would make our home more bearable to live in, if we had children.

They say that children can change a person,

I hope that saying was true, because I didn't see how I was going to spend the rest of my life this way.

I wasn't ready to have a baby and certainly not with Matthew, as much as I have always wanted children I wanted them with James.

I knew that having this baby with Matthew would tie me to him forever.

But I was more scared that he would treat our child the way he treated me, and I wouldn't stand for it.

August 11th

I was really surprised how happy Matthew became when I told him about the baby.

"He was actually sweet to me which made me feel guilty, I felt like Matthew could be a good husband if he knew his wife wasn't in love with his brother, but I have tried I couldn't help it, I have been in love with James since I was a little girl, and I thought he loved me too, but I guess I was mistaken.

Because if he loved me like he so many times told me he did, he wouldn't have ran off with another girl, just because I wouldn't leave my parents and run away with him.

I wish I could get over James and fall in love with Matthew, my life would be so much easier especially with a baby coming, and I wanted my child to feel love in our home.

Chapter Fifteen

Martha came into the shop all giddy with smiles. "Why are you so happy?" I asked her.

"Oh Ally, have you talked to Ann?" "No why?"

"They are moving back home!" "Are you serious?"

"Yes, she said she would call you today, but I can't help it, I can't hold it in, she knows her mother can't keep a secret" she laughed.

"Okay, fill me in on what you know." I was getting so excited about my friend moving back.

"She called me and her father last night she said she got a job offer over on west lane.

My babies are moving back."

I wondered how Tony feels about moving here." I said.

"He is going to work with daddy, and they are going to stay with us until they find a house, I'm so happy." Martha actually beamed with happiness.

"I'm so happy I will have my dear friend back, so should I act surprised when she calls me?"

"Yes please, but I have a feeling she will see right thought that, she knows her mother too well."

"I will do my best acting." I told her.

"I'm going to run over to the B&B on my lunch break, Can you handle things here?" " Of course, I can." She said.

Carla was just checking in a couple, when I walked in, so I took a seat until she was finished.

"Hey Ally, did you come to rent a room?"

"No I'm coming to invite you and Joe to go out to dinner and bowling with Jase and me tonight."

"Me and Joe?, I can't answer for Joe, but I would love to go with you two, I don't know what my brother has told you, but I'm not dating Joe, he is just a guest here.

"I know that, but Jase has asked him already and he said he would love to go so we will pick you up at six."

I turned to walk out the door before she could argue. But there was no argument, she just smiled and said okay I will see you at six.

At the restaurant it was cute, almost like being with very shy teenagers, they didn't talk much so Jase and I had to fill in.

At the bowling lanes, they both made a lot of mistakes, it was funny to watch them, Jase kept looking at me and rolling his eyes, and I would hit him to let him know, he better be nice, but I wanted to laugh out loud.

After we dropped Carla off, Jase drove me home.

"So do I get to come in and see this house that you hate?"

"Sure." I said.

Inside he looked around the house with amazing in his eyes.

"Ally, you have no idea what you have here, I don't know how much your father paid for this house, but I can tell you this much, because I have remodeled a lot of these houses and this house could be worth a lot of money especially in this neighborhood."

"So what exactly are you saying?"

"I'm saying with a little remodeling this place could be beautiful."

And the asking price would go up, you would really be surprised."

"So what about that contractor you told me about, do you think he might be interested in the job?" I said as I put my arms around him.

"Oh I know he would be". Jase said.

After Jase went home I took a bath and went to bed.

She was standing at the end of the hall in her long old fashion dress, she was very beautiful, she had dark hair, but there was saddest in her eyes.

"I would never leave my momma or my child, I need you to find out and prove it, I was a good daughter, and I didn't leave."

Then I woke up again to the sweet smell of baby powder.

I wrote down what she said, comparing my notes I could see that now she was telling me so much more, I wish I could talk to her.

But I think what she wants me to look at is her diary that is where I will find what happened to her. I'm almost sure now that Olivia was visiting me in my dreams.

I have decided to talk to Jase about what has been happening and about my dreams. I just hoped he wouldn't think I was crazy.

Chapter sixteen

Jase these are beautiful, what's the occasion?" I asked as I admired the dozen roses he gave me.

"The occasion is that I love you

Ally, you know I'm not big on words and I'm lacking in the romance field,

I won't be that guy that takes you to the big fancy restaurant and gets down on one knee to propose, and then everyone there cheers because that's just not me, but if you will become my wife, I will do everything in my power to make you happy and I will love you with all of my heart for the rest of my life."

Wow! Who says you are not romantic? I will marry you Jase."

I am so very happy you were in the shop that day when my father passed away, because since that day you have been my rock and if it hadn't been for you, I would not be where I am today, I love you with all of my heart, and you make me so happy."

"Ally, you make me so happy, I think about you every day and I just want to take care of you and raise a family with you.

I think I feel in love with you the day I came into the shop , the very first time I had ever saw you, even though it was a very sad day, I believe I was there for a reason.

I believe I was there to meet my wife."

I put my arms around his necks.

"I love you Jase." "I love you Ally"

"Can you close the shop early tomorrow, we could drive out to my folks, so they can meet you and we can tell them."

"Sure if you want, that will be fine."

"Okay I will call them when I get home."

"Well thank you for the flowers I'm going to go find a vase, have a seat, I will be right back."

As I looked for a vase for the flowers, I got a little nervous wondering how I was going to start this conversation without sounding nuts.

But I knew now I had to tell him.

After I placed the flowers on the table I asked Jase if he wanted a cup of coffee.

"Sure" he came into the kitchen, and sat at the table, Wow these flowers are pretty."

After I got our coffee I sat down across from him, Jase, we need to talk."

"Okay, this sounds serious, are you dumping me, or have you already changed your mind about marrying me, because you know you have to at least give a twenty four notice."

"You are funny, I'm not dumping you, but when I'm finished talking, you may dump me."

"Jase, when my father got sick and I came home to help him run the shop, well the very first night in this house alone while my dad was in the hospital, I had a dream, it was about a young girl standing at the end of the hall and in a whisper she said

"I would never do that to my parents." And that was it.

But when, I woke up, there was a faint smell of baby powder.

So I just chalked it up as a dream and didn't give it much more thought."

He just looked at me and waited to hear the rest of my story.

"But unfortunately the dreams didn't stop there

But have progressed into something more than just a dream I believe the young woman in my dreams is trying to tell me something."

"Wow! So how often do you have this dream, and is it the same dream every time?

It is but now she is saying more to me and sometimes I have them every night and then sometimes just a couple times a week...

And yes basically the dreams are the same.

But there is more, remember the diary I found in the vanity at the shop when we was cleaning the old furniture from the storage room?"

"Yes I remember, didn't it have a girl's name on it?"

"Yeah, it was Olivia, Jase, I don't know how the dreams and the diary connect but they do, I'm really convinced the girl in my dreams is Olivia."

"Wow and why do you think that?" He asked.

"Because some of the thing written in the diary is the same words she says in the dreams.

She keeps telling me to look and I would find it.

Now she says she would never do that to her momma or her child and she would never leave; she says she was a good daughter, almost the same thing Olivia says in her diary."

"Okay could it be possible? By you, reading the diary it could be causing the dreams to progress.

I'm sure you are reading before you go to bed, so it could be just dreams and nothing more, because we know dreams are sometimes caused by what is on our mind or what we eat before we go to sleep."

"Okay but what if that is not the case and this girl is trying to tell me something and that is why I found the diary?"

"So is that what you believe?"

"It is. I really believe she is Olivia, and she is trying to tell me something."

"So do you feel like if you move out of this house the dreams will stop?"

"I don't know. I feel like what I need to do is find out about Olivia and to do that I need to find out where that furniture came from

Maybe, there is a family member that can tell me about Olivia, and what became of her."

"Well, did your father keep records when He would buy items?"

"Yes I think he did, I do know there are books where there are a lot of our items listed."

"Then it shouldn't be hard to find where it came from and I will help you."

"You will? So you don't think I'm crazy?"

"Of course I don't think you are crazy, I mean I don't believe in this kind of stuff, but I do believe in you.

Chapter Seventeen

Carla was very happy when we told her we were getting married.

"I knew you two would end up together, and I couldn't be happier, I have always wanted a sister."

She gave me a hug, 'welcome to the family"

"Thank you' I said.

I really wish I could go with you two I miss my family, I know there are not that many miles between us, but it just seems I never have enough time to make the trip."

"Well Jase is going to hire someone, so you can have more days off" I told her.

"Oh it's not my brother's fault, he has tried to hire someone else before, but I talked him out of it, but now I'm ready for some more days off."

Jase walked in the room to hear that last statement.

"My big sister is in love." He joked.

"That's right I am, and who knowns maybe soon you will be coming to my wedding."

That will great, I'm so glad you found someone to make you happy Sis."

"Me to, Joe is perfect for me, we have fun together and I really care for him."

"I know you do in fact I have known it for some time now, you thought you were hiding it, but it was very obvious that you two have been quite smitten with each other."

The drive there was nice I was actually looking forward to meeting his family.
Jase told me all about them.
He had two younger brothers, still living at home,
Adam and Carson, Carla was his only sister
They were a close net family always spend the holidays together, his dad was retired, his mom was a nurse.

They all made me feel very welcome.
"Jase, you did real good she is beautiful," his dad said as soon as we walked into the kitchen where he was preparing a meal.
His dad gave Jase a big hug and then he gave me a hug "welcome to our home Ally." "Thank you." I said.
"Your mother will be home soon, she is all excited to hear about your engagement.
His brothers were very funny and I could tell they loved and missed their big brother.
They gave him hugs. I had never seen a family that expressed so much love for each other, and I was so happy to be marrying into this loving family.
Everyone was sad that Carla couldn't come with us today.

Jase went to meet his mom at the door when she came home.

"Jase, Oh I have missed you so much"

His mother reminded me of Carla, she was so sweet to me and very excited that we were getting married.

She said she wanted to help anyway we needed her.

After a short visit we drove back home, promising to let them know as soon as we sit our wedding date.

On the way home we talked about it and decided on a June wedding and having it outside on the grounds at the B&B, it was very big and pretty there, we could sit up tents for the reception.

I thought it was a great idea.

The following week Jase and I was invited to Martha and Pete's for dinner, we decided to take this opportunity to tell them we were engaged.

Marth had told me many times how much she liked Jase, so I knew she would be happy for us.

"Martha, you outdid yourself, this food is delicious, and how come you never bring this kind of food to the shop for my lunch?" Jase was always joking with Martha.

"Because you, are not ever at the shop." She said.

"Well I would be there every day if this kind of food was there."

Jase and I have some news." I said to change the subject.

They both just looked at us. "we are getting married in June."

"Oh honey, that is wonderful, I'm so happy for you two, Have you told Ann Yet?

"No I haven't."

"Ally, you know you better tell Ann right away, because you know I can't keep a secret" we both laughed.

I did call Ann when I got home, she was very happy for me.

She already knew that she would be my maid of honor without asking her, I told her we would go over the details of the wedding as soon as I had some plans.

The next day Jase and I went thought Dad's books and after a few hours, we found it, I was so happy, because this could mean solving this mystery and ending these dreams that have been robbing me of my sleep.

"It says he got it from a realtor, Walter Reed in Columbus, Georgia.

"Wow, why would my father go all the way to Columbus, Georgia to buy furniture?"

That is a long ways. "A least eight hours by car." Jase said

And my hopes were shattered.

"Thank you Jase, for helping me" "You are welcome, but we are not done;

Now we have to go to Georgia that is if you want me to go with you?"

"Really, you mean we can go that far to try to find something I'm not even sure what it is I'm looking for"

"Absolutely we can," "Oh Jase, thank you."

And Of course I want you to go with me."

"Okay, whenever you want to go. Just let me know."

"Let's go on our honeymoon."

"Sounds good to me." he said.

I had planned on not reading anymore of Olivia's diary, but I just had to know, so after getting settled in bed, I reached into my night stand and took the diary out, carefully opening the yellowing pages I continued.

August 15th

Matthew told me after supper today, we would go to his parent's house to tell them the news, I wonder if it would make a difference on how they felt about me.

Maybe they would see that I was trying to make my marriage to Matthew work and we were starting our family.

Just maybe they would not talk to me like I was their enemy, but soon to be the mother to their grandchild.

I couldn't understand why they had to always wear that tough exterior look on their face.

August 16th

Matthew's parents were very happy they were going to be grandparents, they congratulate Matthew, like I had nothing to do with it, I heard Matthew tell them that I was going to make a good mother. I know he felt bad at the way they were treating me, his mother's reply was "I sure hope so."

I mean they weren't mean to me, they just ignored me like I wasn't there, which was fine with me because I didn't want to be there.

I hoped they didn't treat their grandchild the way they treated me, these people acted like they didn't know how to love or to be kind to one another.

Maybe that's the reason Matthew is the way he is, but James was never like that, he was kind and sweet and apparently a liar and a cheater.

September 2nd

Matthew has been very kind to me since I told him I was pregnant I told him tomorrow I wanted to spend the day with my mom, he said that was fine, we could just have left overs for supper.

I was so surprised and thought that maybe this baby will change him. Because I believed that I could come to care for Matthew if he wasn't so mean.

I wanted a happy home for my child's sake.

I didn't want it to grow up in an environment the way Matthew did but I wanted our baby to know and to show kindness.

September 3rd

I had a nice visit with momma, she was already making baby blankets for her soon to be grandchild.

"Olivia, can I ask you a question, without you getting upset with me" She said.

"Of course you can Momma."

"Do you love Matthew now?" "I'm not in love with Matthew, but I'm learning to respect him." 'Do you still have feelings for James?" she asked.

"Yes Momma, I do and I can't help it, I do try to forget him and I know now that James never loved me and it still hurts me, but I'm learning to put him in the past and to work on my future with Matthew."

I knew my words made her happy, I couldn't forever hold a grudge toward my parents when I knew I was also to blame.

September 23rd

My book of thoughts have been put on hold, I have been busy

Matthew decided we need a bigger house, I didn't agree but I didn't have a say so in it...

I hated the thought of leaving my parents I would know no one In North Carolina, and my parents wouldn't be around the baby, Matthew knew how unhappy I was about moving to another state.

When I would express my feelings on the matter he would just say it was time for me to outgrow my parents that he was my family now him and our child.

He told me I had been spending too much time at my parent's home.

"But Matthew I will stop going over there so much, please I don't want to move to n Carolina.

"Olivia, we are moving, I have already brought a house, and you will learn to like it there.

We will leave on the train in a few days and you can see the house.

In the meantime this conversation is over.

You didn't really think you could live next door to your parents forever did you?"

September 29th

I tried again to talk Matthew out of moving but my words landed on deaf ears...

Momma and poppa were so disappointed and I couldn't blame them

I didn't need this kind of pleasure being pregnant it was almost like he didn't want our parents around us anymore.

Matthew and I went to Charlotte North Carolina by train

I really enjoyed the train ride it was my first time, I did get a little sick but I managed to hide it from Matthew.

Matthew was taking me to show me the house he had purchased.

But I had already made up my mind to hate it.

We spend two nights on the train. Because of the many stops the train had to make I would have enjoyed it if I wasn't pregnant.

October 2nd

As I look around my new house, I thought it was indeed beautiful but I couldn't appreciate its beauty because of the sadness I was feeling moving away from my parents.
Couldn't Matthew see I needed my mother now more than ever, who was going to be with me when I had our child?
I didn't know how to take care of a newborn I was counting on her to help.
I had peace of mind knowing she was only a few houses down from me.
But here in this big house I would be all alone and what if Matthew was at work when I went into labor.

November 22nd

We got all moved in yesterday, and I'm taking a break from unpacking.

Matthew has left for his new job today and I hoped he hated it so maybe we could go back home, this house is so big we don't have enough things to fill it but Matthew said in time we would

I felt at ease when I can feel the movement of my baby, my heart sings just to know that in two months I will hold my baby and I will never feel alone again.

When I expressed my concerns to Matthew about when the baby comes, he said he would find a midwife for me I was glad, not as glad as I would be if I had my mother but still I wouldn't be alone.

I even asked Matthew if my mother could come stay with me until after the baby was born.

He told me to grow up and stop acting like I was a baby that I had let go of my mother.

November 23rd

I miss my parents so badly, Matthew knew how sad I was, but he didn't care how I felt.
How was I support to fall in love with a man that was so arrogant.

Only two more months my love and I get to hold you in my arms.
It is so strange how you can have so much love for someone, you have never met.
I asked Matthew the other day if he wanted to feel the baby move.
He said. He will feel the movement when he or she is born.
I so hoped when the baby is born he will love it.
Matthew is such a hard person just like both of his parents; he never shows any kind of emotion than anger

November 24th

Matthew just informed me that his family was coming for thanksgivings, which was in three days. I'm not happy today.

I was also told that he wanted the house spotless and he even gave me the menu he wanted for the thanksgiving meal.

Matthew acted like he either wanted to please his patents very much or he was scared of them I didn't know which it was.

I couldn't wait for Thanksgiving to be over...

Now his family wouldn't be leaving when the meal was over but they would be staying for three days.

November 28th

I can't believe I'm writing this, but here it goes.

I was so very happy Matthew's parents came for thanksgiving.

The meal was perfect but the best thing of all was they told Matthew how upset they were that he moved their soon to Be grandchild so far away and they wanted him to move back before the baby was born.

I asked them where we would live. His father informed me that Matthew did not sell our house, it was still standing empty.

Matthew told them that he had been thinking about it for some time now, but I didn't believe him, I just knew how much he wanted to please his parents.

"Well boy stop thinking about it and do it." His father ordered.

I was so happy but I acted like I was unconcerned about what they were talking about because just like Matthew they didn't care about my opinion, and I thought if maybe I was happy about moving back they all would decide maybe it wasn't a good idea, but inside I was about to bust, just to think about being near momma again made me so happy.

And if we moved very soon momma could be with me when my time came I knew it would be a lot of work but we could do it.

I had to try with all of my might not to say one word about moving back before the baby was born.

His parents had already said that so I just had to wait and see if it happened and hoped.

November 30th

Matthew's parents left for home this morning and I was glad

Matthew is at work and I have the house to myself at last a little peace. I feel my precious baby kicking inside of me, only seven more weeks.

Before his dad left this morning, he told Matthew he would open up and air the house out for him, Matthew didn't say anything.

When his mother hugged him goodbye, I heard her tell him "see you real soon son." She hugged me goodbye but I could tell it was forced I know she didn't want to.

His Dad just said to me, "take care of my grandchild."

December 3rd

We got word today that my poppa was very sick and I needed to return home.

The train seemed to take a long time to get there I was so worried about my father. He had always been so healthy.

When I got home, Poppa was in bed and there was a nurse with him.

"Oh Olivia, I'm so glad you came, your father has been asking for you" my momma said...

I went into the room, my heart sank this is not the man I had just seen a few months ago. He was pale and thin.

"Poppa, I'm here" he told the nurse he wanted to speak to me alone. Once she was out of the room he looked at me and said.

"Olivia I'm so sorry I made you marry Matthew, it was wrong, I should have let you marry the man you loved.

"Poppa it's okay, don't worry about that now."

"No Olivia, I kept the letters from you and I lied to you when I told you that girl's father told me James had run away with his daughter, I knew that James had joined the service and I knew he was coming back for you, will you please forgive me?"

I was speechless I couldn't believe what he had just told me But I knew I had to forgive him, he was my father and I loved him.

"Yes Poppa, I forgive you, rest now."

"Olivia, your mother didn't know I lied to you so please be kind to her, you have always been a good daughter."

"Poppa please rest now, you don't need to talk anymore."

I could see by him talking it was taking a lot out of him.

December 7th

My Poppa died in his sleep today, my heart is broken and I'm so worried about my momma, I needed to be with her But after the funeral, Matthew had insisted we come back home.

Matthew helped me today to paint the baby's room,

We painted it a soft gray at Matthew's request.

I wanted to wait to see if I was having a boy or girl.

Before we did the room, but I was learning it didn't really matter what I wanted.

I was so tired all the time and my feet were swollen, I was ready to have the baby, my midwife had come and checked on me two times I really liked her she was kind.

December 10th

I had just finished supper dishes when Matthew walked into the kitchen. He asked me how I felt about moving back to Columbus.

I was scared to answer truthfully, so I said.

"Well Matthew, you know I miss my mother and I worry about her but wherever you are that is where I will be, so the decision is yours.

"I know the decision is mine, I'm the husband, I was just asking you what you thought." He snapped at me.

"Matthew, why do you have to talk to me so hateful?"

He didn't answer he just walked out of the room.

It was like living with Jekyll and Hyde.

December 12th

Yesterday Matthew told me we were moving back to Columbus, so all day I have been packing, I'm so happy.
It has been hard on me to get everything packed up.
Matthew came home and told me to just pack my bag that we were taking the train home and that he had hired some guys to bring our things.
What a happy day it was for me, I sent word to the midwife I would no longer need her services I was going home to be with my mother.
I knew the train ride would be long but I didn't care.
I knew it was his parents that wanted us home before the baby came and I also knew if it hadn't been for them Matthew would have never moved back.
So I had a lot to thank them for, I just couldn't let them know that.

December 20th

Momma came over to help me get everything unpacked and put things away.

It was so good to be with her again.

I told her how much I had missed her.

Matthew told me we could wait until after the baby was born to fix up the baby's room, I thought that made better sense, but of course I didn't say that.

He acted like it bothered him that my mother was here helping me, but he didn't say anything.

I had everything I needed for the baby after Matthew brought home his old baby bed from his parent's house, I wasn't crazy about it but momma and I got it all cleaned up and it looked decent enough, Momma helped me make some baby clothes and Matthew let me go shopping to buy what else I needed.

December 26th

What a great Christmas, we had. My mother and Matthew's parents came to Christmas dinner, they even treated me with respect, I'm sure it was because Momma was there, but I didn't care, it was a nice Christmas.

Momma had helped me cook the dinner and his parents had brought me things for the baby, it was real nice.

I was starting to think maybe this child was bringing everybody together and it wasn't even born yet.

I missed Poppa today and I know Momma did to.

This was our first Christmas without him.

And I was saddened to know that he would never meet his grandchild.

December 27th

I woke early today so I could finish putting things away. Matthew was off of work for a few days because of Christmas he went back to his old Job here.

He told me that he wishes he hadn't sold his business but he said he was going under but he said one day he would own his business again.

He didn't like to have a boss over him, and I could definitely see that in him.

Matthew never talked to me unless it was to throw out orders and I was surprised he was telling me this. I knew he wasn't happy.

Matthew married me knowing I didn't love him and he also knew I didn't want to marry him.

I know he hoped my feelings would change over time, but they haven't.

I want to make a home for my child, but my heart will always belong to James now and forever.

December 29th

Matthew told me yesterday he was not selling the house in N. Carolina but had purchased yet another one a few houses down from it, he said one day we would move back there, I hoped that day would never come..

I was happy being close to my mother, I was the only one she had now since Poppa has passed away, she needed me and I needed her, I knew it would break her heart if she couldn't be around her grandchild.

Matthew didn't say anything to me anymore about me spending my time there, so when he left for work I was at her house or she was at my house.

It made my life with Matthew bearable.

We mostly talked while we sew baby clothes.

I never treated Matthew bad, I tried to show kindness toward him, but it was hard when he would be mean to me for no reason, it was almost like he had this angrier inside of him and he took it on me

December 30th

I woke up today with a backache and it was hard to fix Matthew's breakfast but I still had to when I told him I was having pains in my back, he seemed unconcerned and sat there waiting for me to put his food on the table.

I would spend the day with momma today after my work was done.

Once at her house the pain wasn't as bad she said my body was getting prepared for birth, I told her I was scared but she reassured me everything would be fine, I don't know what I would do without her.

She gave me comfort, she also made me a cup of tea and rubbed my back, by the time I went home I felt so much better, she had offered to cook our supper for me since I wasn't feeling good, but I told her no, I knew Matthew would not like that at all, he thought it was my job as a wife to do it all by myself.

I cooked Matthew a good supper and I got things ready just in case this baby decided to come early,

The fact was the correct due date was more of a guess anyway.

I was going to be a good mother to my child and I would never force her or him into a marriage.

I wanted them to know what being love was all about.

I had asked my mother one time if she had ever been in love and she was very honest with me.

She said yes she had when she was a young girl before Poppa.

But he was killed in a farming accident.

She said she never got over him but placed him in a part of her heart that only belonged to him.

I thought that was what I had to do with James.

December 31st

I knew something wasn't right when I got out of bed this morning so I asked Matthew if he could ask my Mother to come spend the day with me while he was at work, because I thought maybe I might be going into labor.

"You are not due for two more weeks, it's probably because you have been eating all of those sweets your momma brought over, after you have this baby, you will stop eating the way you have been."

"But Matthew, maybe it's not, I'm scared."

He just walked out the door, he was so hateful, Why did he even want to be with me? I'm sure he doesn't love me, no more than I love him, so why were we together? I thought.

Momma is here, thank you Jesus.

Throughout the day, the pain got worst, I thought I was dying, I could tell it was hard on momma to see me in pain we both prayed the baby would come soon.

At some point Matthew came home he came into the room to ask me if I wanted him to go get his mother, I told him no, unless she could take this pain away, I didn't men to snap at Matthew but at this point I didn't care if he got mad.

I didn't want Matthew or his overbearing mother in the room with me.

I just wanted this to be over.

Almost fifteen hours later it was over and I held my beautiful daughter in my arms, Momma and I both were crying, I think Momma was crying because it was over and her daughter was no longer in pain, and I cried because my daughter was in my arms, and I already loved her so much.

Matthew came into the room after Momma had the baby cleaned up and she was wrapped in her new blanket.

January 1st 1908

Well little one, you were almost a New Year baby, if you would have waited just two hours but I'm glad you are here my darling, I kissed her cheek.

Matthew instantly fell in love with his daughter, maybe the first person he has ever really loved.

He named her Mary after his mother, again I wasn't asked.

But Mary was fine with me, because she was my Mary.

Because it was so late I asked momma to spend the night, I was so tired I needed her to help me with baby.

January 12th

Momma helps me out a lot with Mary.

I'm glad Matthew doesn't mind that I and the baby spend a lot of time at her house,

She is crazy about her granddaughter, they are so cute together.

I'm always home and have supper on the table before Matthew comes home, I don't want to give him a reason to not let me go to Momma's every day, she helps me every day to clean the house and have the Landry done and if Matthew knew I'm sure that would upset him.

He just didn't understand that my mother needed to be needed it gave her joy to tend to Mary.

Since Mary was born, his mother has come over two times and both times she has only held the baby for a few minutes before handing her back to me. she just wasn't a motherly person.

March 8th

Matthew insisted I lose weight and I'm trying but it's hard when your mother is a great cook.

But I have been watching what I eat and so has Matthew.

At the dinner table he watches to see how much food I put on my plate, and I don't dare to go for seconds of anything, and no dessert for me at all,

But when I'm at my momma's I eat what I want and still the weight is coming off.

Mary is a good baby she already sleeps through the night.

Every evening after supper Matthew leaves the house, he never tells me where he is going, he only says. "Going out, be back later.

I know I should care that my husband leaves every evening, but I don't care but just the opposite.

While he is gone, Mary and I can spend time with Momma.

April 7th

Matthew caught me writing in my book yesterday I was so scared he would read it so I hid it in my vanity I can never let him see it.

He didn't say anything just looked at it.

He must have seen the terrifying look on my face.

I will have to be a lot more careful from now on.

I even thought about destroying my book of thoughts.

Chapter Eighteen

I closed the book, wow that was close, I knew Matthew hadn't found the diary because if he had, I wouldn't be reading it right now, I had to stop reading, because my eyes lids were getting heavy and to tomorrow was a big day because Ann and her family would be here.

I missed Martha at the shop, but knew she wanted to be with her grandsons now, and I didn't blame her.

But her replacement Lee was a hard worker and he knew a lot about Antiques.

He had worked for my father at his other antique shop so I was really happy to have him; he made my life a lot easier.

Jase came by as I was locking up, I asked him to go with me to Martha and Pete's to visit with Ann and her husband, I wanted Tony and Jase to become friends.

"Hey, you ready?" "Yes I'm ready and I'm so excited. I said as I gave Jase a big hug.

On the drive over I filled Jase in on Ann and her husband.

How they met, where they moved to.

"Pete opened the door for us.

"Ann has been waiting all day to see you Ally."

"Ally, I have missed you so much" she said hugging me a little too tight. I started to laugh.

"Ann, I'm so happy, you have moved back, this town just wasn't the same without you girl" I gave her a hug, and then I introduced Jase to Tony.

Jase, do you remember Ann?" " Yes, I remember you, he shook her hand, and believe me I know everything about you, Ally talks about her best friend at least every day."

"Oh Ann, never stops talking about Ally."

We still had our arms around each other.

"Oh you guys are just jealous" Ann said.

"Oh my goodness look how big you guys are, the last time I seen you two, you were so small"

The boys came out of the kitchen with Martha.

They were identical twins and they were adorable.

"How do you tell them apart?" Jase asked.

"We just say their names and wait to see who answers." Tony joked.

I thought I would try that.

"Hi Logan" when Logan shyly said" Hi" I knew the other one was Landon. "Hi Landon, how are you?" he turned his face toward his mom so I couldn't see his face, they were so cute.

I bet your grandma was happy to see you two guys.

"Yes their grandma was." Martha said.

While the boys played, we sat in the living room and talked about the wedding.

"So have you two decided where you are having the ceremony yet?"

Martha asked.

"We are going to have it at the B&B, we thought we would rent a big white tent and have the reception in that, but the ceremony could take place outside on the gazebo, Jase said he would paint it white and it's very large so I think it will be perfect." I said.

"Oh that does sounds nice, you could decorated it with crepe paper rose balls and vines and flowers, with just simple white soft lights, draped in white tulle, it will so pretty" Ann sounded so excited.

"It sounds beautiful, Okay Ann; you are in charge of decorating the gazebo." I told her.

"I would love to do that, oh you won't be sorry you put me in charge of it, I promise.

Jase, mom mentioned that you owned the sandcastle B&B.

That place is beautiful now, we drove by it on the way into town." " Thank you" Jase said.

"Wait until you see the Antique shop, it is nothing like the last time you seen it, it is beautiful." Martha told Ann.

"I have to come by tomorrow and see it, I have heard so much about it, since Jase redid it."

"I'm there all day tomorrow," I told her.

"So have you found your wedding dress yet?" "No I had to wait for my best friend to help me." "Girl we have to go shopping soon, June is just around the corner." "I know your right we need to start getting things ready.

"Okay I have two weeks before I start my job, what day is good for you?'

"The shop is closed on Tuesdays and Sundays." I answered.

"Tuesday, we go find you a dress," "and you a dress also" I said.

"I will check with Jase's sister Carla to make sure she can go on Tuesday,"

Martha spoke up "Don't worry about the food, daddy and I talked about it and this will be our wedding gift to you, all I need from you two is what you want us to serve.

'Thank you so much, that is very kind of you both."

"And it takes one more thing off of our list" Jase said.

We visited for a while longer, Jase took me back to the shop to get my car.

I gave Jase a kiss good night, than I drove home.

After I was settled in bed,

I reached for the diary.

Even though I was tired, I felt like I was so involved in Olivia's life I just had to find out more of what she was going through.

It was like I knew her and Matthew and James, and I was so hoping I would read the part that her and James lived happy ever after.

I thought about her throughout the day.

I wondered if the people who had lived here before my father
Had ever had dreams and what could it be that Olivia wants me to find, I wanted to talk to Ann about it, but I knew she wouldn't believe that my dreams meant what I thought they meant, she would just say they were just dreams., but I knew now that wasn't the case.
Dad had mentioned that this house was empty and off of the market for many years now I wondered why?
I remember seeing this house, but there are a lot of Victorian house on this side of town, so I never really thought much about this house, I didn't pay that much attention when Dad said one day he would own it.

July 5th

I have stopped writing in my thoughts book, I was so scared Matthew would catch me again, so I just stopped and have kept it hid away.

For the last year I'm convinced Matthew has a Lady friend.

Mary is getting so big, she is the light of my world, and Matthew is constantly showering her with gifts,

Mary and I still spend a lot of time at my mother's house, I feel peace when I'm there, and the truth is I wish we could live there.

I hate it at home, because it doesn't feel like home to me.

And Matthew has gotten worst, he yells at me a lot and a few times he hits me when I'm not expecting it.

I had to walk on eggshells when Matthew was home, I was glad he had started spending his nights somewhere else, sometimes it was late when he came home.

I knew better to ask where he had been.

August 18th

Matthew told me today, he wanted another child.

I could not understand why, Matthew didn't love me.

I wasn't ready to have another baby, Matthew did love Mary but he never spends time with her.

"Matthew, I'm not reading to have a child right now."

"Look Olivia, I'm not crazy about having another baby right now, but my mother says it's not good for a kid to grow up alone without a sibling and I agree with her."

"Matthew, this is not your mother's decision."

I was getting very upset.

"You are right Olivia, it is not my mother's decision, it is mine, and I want another child."

"Well I'm sorry Matthew, but I think I have a say in this, And I'm not ready to have another baby."

I walked out of the room leaving him with a blank look on his face.

"He followed me into the other room.

"What did you just say to me, did you just give me an order?"

"I didn't answer him, I just started folding clothes.

"This conversation is not over!" he said as he walked out the door.

October 20th

I'm so unhappy, I don't know how long I can stay with Matthew, when I talk to Momma about it she tells me I have to stay with him, he is my husband.

If it wasn't for Mary, I would run far away but I know Matthew would never let Mary leave and I would never leave without her.

Matthew has gotten more and more demanding.

He thinks I should jump whenever he speaks, now he tells me that when he is gone out for the evening he wants Mary at home not at my mothers.

So I told him fine, momma can come here and visit while he is out.

He said I needed to stop spending so much time with my mother.

I know it's just a matter of time before he tells me she can no longer come over.

I think Matthew is having an affair and I hope he is, so maybe he will fall in love with her and leave me.

November 19th

Yesterday, something happened that made me stop and examine my whole life, a life I have been living to please everyone living my life in misery just so I could be this good daughter, but no more, I let men control me and deny me love and happiness.,, I let them steal away my life and my happiness.

I was in Momma and poppa's bedroom looking for a picture of me when I was Mary's age to see if we looked alike, but what I found had me running for home, in the top of their closet was a small tin box thinking there might be pictures in it, I took it down and opened it only to discover many letters addressed to me from James.

This is what My Poppa meant when he said he kept the letters from me.

Because he was so sick I thought he was just confused at what he was saying.

I took the letters out of the box went back into the living room and got Mary, I told momma I would talk to her later and went home while she stood there looking at me.

Once home I hid the letters in my secret drawer in the vanity.

I would have to wait until after supper and Matthew has gone out for the night.

I couldn't concentrate on the meal I was trying to prepare my mind was on James's letters, I wanted to rush dinner and rush Matthew out the door.

But of course everything went in slow motion it seemed.

November 26th

Once Matthew left I put Mary to bed and behind a locked door, I read the first letter.
It was dated shorty after that day his sister told me he had ran away with Abigail.

Dear Olivia, my love, please forgive me, but I had to leave .my parents told me it was best that I get my life together before we are to be married , they said right now that I was no good for you, so to prove them wrong and to show them I can change. I joined the service, I will write to you every day. And when I get out we can marry.
Matthew and my parents told me they would wait and give me a chance to change. They told me they understood that you didn't love Matthew, but that you and I were in love. I love you my darling. James.

I put that letter in the drawer and took out the second one. My father had told me that James had joined the server, why hadn't I heard what he was saying to me.

But it wouldn't have mattered anyway, the damage was already done. I was married to Matthew.

Dear Olivia, I really hope you are not upset with me for leaving without saying goodbye, but I didn't have time.

Olivia I love you so much, please say you will wait for me, Matthew told me he was dating a girl from North Carolina, I'm glad for him, so that means he will stay away from you.

When I get home for Christmas, we can make our wedding plans; I can't wait to spend the rest of my life with you... Love you always James.

Dear Olivia, my mother wrote me and told me you and Matthew were married yesterday

She said you have grown very close to Matthew and couldn't help but fall in love with him.

Olivia, I know it is my fault.

I should have never left you there with Matthew

I can't say I'm happy for you, because right now my heart is being torn from my chest.

I will always love you. James

November 30th

After the fifth letter, I knew James thought I didn't love him anymore And I had married Matthew because I fell in love with him, why did my parents rob me from my love and my happiness,

Dear Olivia,, I won't write to you anymore, I know this is my fault, I should have never listened to Matthew or my parents, I should have never left you,, you will always be my love even if you are now my sister n law, I will never stop loving you...... James.

I grieved over what could have been.

James was and always will be my only love, and I knew if I had the chance again on the day he had asked me to run away with him I would have did it, we were both treated very unfair by both of our families, and it was us that was paying the price.

December 2nd

I couldn't take the chance of Matthew finding the letters so I took them back to my momma's and confronted her

"How could you keep these letters from me? I married Matthew because I was trying to please you, because I wanted to be a good daughter.

You robbed me from being happy now 'I'm in a marriage with a man I will never love.

She just looked at me, momma had tears in her eyes; I walked out of their house.

Chapter Nineteen

I Closed the diary, I couldn't believe her parents kept James's letters from her, how sad.

I laid there thinking about Olivia until I fell asleep.

Ann came to the shop the next day, and she loved it.

"This is so pretty and you are right it doesn't even resemble what I remember, do you get a lot of business now?"

"Yes we do." "Wow, look at you, you own a beautiful antique store, and soon a great B&B, your life is going good."

She walked around the shop looking at all the rooms.

"Oh my goodness I can't believe this is the same place we use to hang out in when we were kids, what a change.

"All thanks to Jase." I said.

"After we are married, he wants to do the same thing to my house."

"Oh wow, that will be really nice, I'm so happy for you Ally."

"Thank you Ann, did you ever image us moving back here?"

"No not in a million years, we were so determined to get out of this town."

"Well I'm so very glad you are back here, I have missed you so much."

I was glad Ann didn't mention my dreams anymore because I didn't want to go into the details of it right now. I had to many others things on my mind.

I had a lot of fun shopping with Ann and Carla.

I found the perfect dress it wasn't full, but a long white slimming dress with a short train. Ann and Carla's dresses were Rose color.

Since Jase told me to decide on the food, we met with Martha after we were done shopping and went over the food choices.

Jase was taking care of the tent and the cake had been ordered, so the only thing I had to do was the flowers and the center pieces for the tables.

I was glad when Jase's parents and brothers arrived at the B&B a few days before our wedding because his mother was a lot of help to me; she made the center pieces for the tables.

Between, her and Martha everything was coming together.

The guys set up the tent, the tables and chairs were set up, Martha and my soon to be mother n law had everything looking beautiful.

I was amazed when we went to our rehearsal.

Ann made the gazebo so elegant, it was beautiful.

After the rehearsal dinner, we finished up the last details.

And I was more than ready to go home. It had been a long day.

After I was bed I took out the diary, I knew I should be sleeping for my big day tomorrow, but when I closed my eyes sleep wouldn't come.

January 2nd

I haven't written in my thought book for a very long time. Mary is growing like a weed, she is a joy, and I can't believe she is already two, she is so smart.

Matthew is treating me a little better since the last time I have put an entry in this book, I have forgiving my momma, and we don't speak of it anymore.

What is done is done, I'm pregnant again.

I didn't want to have another baby with Matthew, but this baby will be loved.

Momma is very happy about it.

When I told Matthew, he didn't say anything.

March 24th

Matthew and his sister will be giving their parents a surprise fortieth wedding anniversary and yes I have wondered if James will be there.

I also wondered how I would act around him.

Would he be alone, or would he have found someone new?

Matthew never speaks of his brother, almost like he doesn't exist.

And I knew better than to bring his name up.

But he was always on my mind, and I didn't think I could stand to see him with someone else.

I don't think my heart could take it.

April 14th

James was at the party I heard because I wasn't there, I suffered a miscarriage, and I stayed in bed while Matthew took Mary to the party; she got to meet her uncle James for the first time.

June 29th

Momma and I went shopping yesterday, we stopped at a café to have lunch, and James walked up to us, my heart leaped.

He looked the same and I found out very fast I still felt the same about him.

Momma excused herself I knew she felt like she owed me this much.

"Hello Olivia, how are you?" He said

"I'm okay, but I have missed you so much." I started to cry.

"Olivia, please don't cry." "I'm sorry,"

Momma was coming back to the table. "Meet me tomorrow evening at our spot" he turned to walk away. "No I can't" but he kept walking.

My hands got so sweaty and my heart was beating very fast.

July 30th

After Matthew left for his night out, I took Mary to Momma, telling her I had to run to the store. I knew she didn't believe me but she didn't say anything, she had watched Mary before while I ran errands.

I was so scared I would get caught but I was just going to tell James, I could never see him again without Matthew because it wasn't right.

As soon as I seen him standing there my heart melted I loved him so much, I went into his arms.

"Oh Olivia, I have dreamed of the day I would hold you in my arms again."

"James, I'm married to your brother and there is nothing we can do to change that" I cried.

I heard a sound and I jumped but James assured me it was nothing, I had a real bad feeling. I told James I could not see him again and I turned and ran.

By the time I got to mommas I was shaking. I had to calm myself down before I went home.

It was so good to be in James's arms again I loved him so much.

I knew there would be hope for us, as much as I wanted to be with him.

I was married to Matthew now.

I know Matthew was spending his evenings with someone else, and I was glad because that was the only hope I had of ever being free from him.

Because I knew I could never leave him, but he could leave me because that is the kind of person he is.

He does what he wants.

August 3rd

Matthew has been acting very strange the last few days Yesterday I was folding clothes and he walked pass me and hit me and knocked me to the bed for no reason, he called me a name.

I was so scared that he knew I had met James.

I vowed as long as I was married to him I would never go to our secret place again.

August 15th

Yesterday while Matthew was at work and Mary was taking a nap, there was a knock on the door, I opened it to see James standing there he handed me a gift.
"James you can't be here" "I know but I had to see you"
I don't want you to think I just left you, Matthew and my parents assured me they would let you know that I had joined the service but I would back soon."
"James, your sister told me you had run off with Abigale and you two were to be married."
"No Olivia, no I would never do that, it has always been you that I love, I hate my family for what they did to us."
"James, you have to go" I told him as I closed the door.
I haven't did anything wrong and I shouldn't have to be this scared.
But because of that fear, I made a big mistake. I left the gift on the table by the door.

When I heard Mary cry, I went to her.

When Matthew came home I seen it and I tried to hide it but he had already seen it.

"What's this? I was so thankful James had not put his name on it.

"Oh just a little gift from momma" I lied, "So open it." He said

I took the package and opened it; it was a small bottle of perfume.

Matthew took it out of my hand and opened the lid and smelled it.

He looked at me for a long time very hateful.

"Throw it in the trash now." 'Okay" I said and started toward the trash. "I want it Mary said in her little voice.

Matthew picked her up. "You don't want that trash' he said.

September29th

Once again for no reason Matthew walked up to me and hit me in the back of my head sending me flying across the floor.

I started to cry. "Matthew what is wrong? Talk to me please."

I begged.

"You think I'm stupid? You think I don't know?"

October 4th

I'm scared I don't know what Matthew is going to do next, I was convinced he knew I went to see James, what else could he have meant by his words.
I thought about telling him what had happened that I just went to tell him I could never see him again without my husband, but I knew Matthew wouldn't believe me.
And I didn't want to take the chance that maybe by some miracle he didn't know.

October 9th

Last night I was awake when I heard Matthew come home but I pretend to be sleeping, he jerked the covers off of me.
He ordered me to get to get out of bed.
I got up and put my rope on, I didn't say anything I just looked at him waiting for him to hit me.
"Why do you drive me crazy?" he said.
"I don't mean to" I answered him." " Are you going behind my back and seeing my brother?" " No Matthew I'm not!"
That is when I felt the first blow, it knocked me backwards, and I fell to the bed.
I tasted the blood on my lip.
"Matthew this has to stop" I screamed at him.
"I'm not seeing James."
"If I ever catch you with James again I will kill you, do you understand me?"

"Yes I understand," I was crying holding my mouth where he had hit me.

December 11th

Matthew has been acting very nice to me since the other night, but I keep my distant from him and only speak to him when I'm asked a question.
I stayed at Momma's house as much as I could..
I was surprised Matthew hadn't said anything to me about it.
He has changed and it worried me.
He talked about taking a trip he said he needed to check on his houses, because he was thinking about putting them for sale.
I was glad because I never wanted to move back there.
He was gone for a week and it was so peaceful here , Momma spend the nights here with me and Mary, I loved it.

December 21st

Matthew said last night that we needed time alone for a few days and that he was taking me away for the weekend right after Christmas.

I don't want to go.

I told him momma couldn't babysit for that long. He said don't worry his mother was caring for her.

But Matthew, you just came home from a trip.

I know and it gave me time to think, that's why I feel like it's a good idea that we get away together for a few days. He told me.

December 22nd

I wish I knew how I could get out of this trip, I'm scared of Matthew.

I took the perfume out of my secret place and smelled it.

"Mommy, daddy said to throw that away, he said Uncle James gave you that, and he don't like it"

"Mary, when did daddy tell you that?" "The day he said throw it in the trash"

"Mary, please don't tell daddy I have this okay because daddy will get very angry, this is our secret okay."

"Okay mommy, I won't tell him."

December 27th

Matthew said he wanted to leave early in the morning, I hated to leave Mary with his parents, I prayed Matthew would change his mind about going tomorrow.

Chapter Twenty

I turned the pages, they were blank, she didn't write another single word

Throughout her writing she would go days and weeks and even a year before, but she always came back to write more, but this time she didn't

That was it, the end of the diary; I couldn't believe I would never find out what happened. I hated this.

Now I will never know what happened to Olivia.

I had a hard time getting to sleep, I was so disappointed.

I guess I just wanted to keep reading and be a part of this young girl's life,

I wanted to help her even though I knew I couldn't because it was back in the 1900, but I wanted a happy ending, but instead I got no ending.

The next morning, I met Ann at the hair saloon, the girl did my hair up, and I really liked it this way.

On the way to the B&B, Ann insisted I eat something but there were so many butterflies in my stomach I was sure there was no room for food, but just to please her, we stopped and got a breakfast sandwich,

Jase's brother's had the white chairs in neat rolls in front of the gazebo...

Everything looked so beautiful, there were lights hanging from trees.

Some of the trees had mason jar with tea lights in them hanging from the branches.

Once Ann and I arrived we carried our things inside to the room that was reserved for us. We would hang out at the B&B until the ceremony which would start at dusk; I had always wanted a moon light wedding

And thanks to my new family and my friends they made it happen for me.

After we put things away, we walked over to the tent where the reception was going to be.

I couldn't ask for a prettier place, I was amazed how everyone pulled together and took a plain white wedding tent and made it so gorgeous.

There was hanging floral garland, draped fabric with soft twinkle lights.

When the DJ guy came in to set up, we went back to our room to rest, because everything was taken care of according to Jase's mother and Martha, and I didn't want to be in there way.

Ann brought up the subject I was really hoping she wouldn't.

"So Ally, are you still having those dreams?"

"Yes I'm still having them, not as often as before."

"Why do you think you are still having them and does Jase know about them?"

"Yes I have talk to him about them""

"What does he think?' "Like you, he doesn't really think much about them but he is supposing."

"Well that's good, Jase is a good man.

We really got lucky to find such good guys."

"Yes we did." Very glad she dropped the subject about the dreams.

Carla came to the room to get dressed, and they both helped me dressed,

I started to get a little nervous as the time started getting closer for us to go outside, Martha came up to check on us.

"There is a lot of people here." She even acted nervous.

The only person that didn't seem nervous was Ann.

As I walked down the aisle to marry the man of my dreams, I thought about my father.

As much as I loved Pete, because he was my second dad I wished I was on my father's arm, I missed him so much and I know he would have been so happy for me today.

Jase looked so handsome.

The wedding and the reception went great. My life was now complete with Jase.

Chapter Twenty One

For our honeymoon, we were going to Georgia to find the answers I was looking for now more than ever.

I couldn't believe I was married to this great guy; my father would have loved Jase.

We left early the next morning in hopes of solving this mystery.

After we were settled in our room and after searching just about all of Columbus phonebook

I finally found Walter Reed's daughter, she gave me her mother's phone number and I felt like

I may have just reached someone that could help me

"Thank you for calling Scott's rentals, how can I help you?"

"Hi my name is Ally and I'm an antique collector in North Carolina, and I have a very old, I'm thinking maybe around the early eighteenth century colonial bedroom suite, and I'm really interested it in and searching my father's records it says he purchased it three years ago at an auction in Columbus Georgia from a Mr. Walter reed."

"Yes that would be my late husband.

He was in real estate and would occasionally auction off household furniture estates."

"Oh I see" I think she heard the disappointment in my voice.

"Maybe if I saw a picture of it, I might be able to help you,

I was usually with my husband at these sales and I myself am a restorer of old furniture though I have never restored something that old."

"Oh that would be wonderful, Could I come by tomorrow?"

'Yes dear we are open eight am until five pm."

"Thank you so much."

"So what did you find out?" Jase said when I got off of the phone.

"She said I could come by tomorrow with a photo of the furniture and she will see if she can help me, she said Mr. Reed was her late husband and he did deal with antique furniture and she helped him, so maybe she will remember this bedroom suite."

"Well I hope so for you honey, so you can put this behind you and we can start to focus on our house.

"I know Jase, I'm sorry but I just need to find out so maybe then I will be able to put this behind me, but I know my dreams are real, and I want to know what happened.

"I believe you think they are real, and I'm here to help you

"Do you want me to go with you tomorrow?"

"Thank you Jase, even though you are being sarcastic, I still want you to go with me."

"I'm sorry Ally, I do believe that the dreams are real to you, but you know I don't believe in things like that."

"I know, but it has been so long now and I'm still having the dreams not so much as before but still I'm having them"

"Well for tonight, let's go out and check out Columbus and supper, I'm starved." Jase said.

The next morning, Jase and I went to visit Mrs. Reed and to show her the photo I had taken of the furniture.

After we introduced our selves to her, I showed her the picture.

She studied it for a while then she said.

"I am almost certain this belonged to the Wilkins estate over on Crawford street, and the reason is I looked at it to bid on it, but decided it would be too much work, I mean I'm not a hundred percent sure, but I know Mrs. Wilkens is in a nursing home. Not far from here, she may be able to tell you more about it, if it belonged to her family."

"I would really appreciate your help." I told her.

After she gave us the address, we thanked her and left.

"Well what do you think?" Jase asked me when we were outside.

"I want to go visit Mrs. Wilkins." "Okay, let's go."

Once we arrived at the nursing home, I asked Jase if it was okay that I go in alone, I felt like maybe she would be more comfortable with just me.

"Sure honey, I will wait in the car, take your time, and good luck, I really hope you get some answers today, I put the diary in my bag and got out of the car, I became nervous as I walked up the sidewall to the front door.

The lady at the front desk was very kind, after I gave her Mrs. Wilkins's name, she became very excited

"Well hello, are you Mary's granddaughter?"

"No ma'am, just a friend." I didn't know what to say.

"Well she is going to be happy to have a visitor." She said.

After she took my name and wrote it down in her book, she walked with me down the long hall.

"Here we are," she opened the door, there was a woman sitting in a wheelchair by the window, the room was small with just a bed, a dresser and nightstand and a television and there was a small bathroom. But it was decorated very nicely

"Mary, you have a visitor today." The lady told her.

I walked over to her. "Hi Mary"

She just looked at me, like she was trying to recognize who I was.

I waited until the lady left us alone before I said anymore.

"Mary, you don't know me, my name is Ally I own an antique shop in Charlotte, North Carolina and I have a bedroom suit that I think may have belonged to your family."

"Why would you think that, Ally?"

Mary must have been over ninety years old but

I knew by the way she spoke there was nothing wrong with her mind.

"I have a photo of it" I said as I took the picture from my bag.

She didn't look at it long before she said. "This belonged to my mother.

My father owned two houses in Charlotte.

"Mary, Can you tell me about your mother?'

"Well I can tell you what I can remember, my mother abandoned me and my father when I was only three years old and I never seen her again."

"What was she like before she left?"

She was a very good mother and I was heartbroken when she left"

Like I said I was only three, so I can't remember a lot.

She ran away with my uncle James, so through the years I become very resentful toward my mother.

After she ran away, my daddy put this furniture in a spare room.

I remember when I was older I asked him if I could use it, because I thought it was so pretty, but he said no.

I knew the reason was because she had admired it one day in a store and my father got it for her it was very expensive and a week later she ran off with his brother, so I didn't blame him, I couldn't understand why he kept it, but he did."

"What about your grandparents?"

My Grandmother lived just two houses down from us and momma and I spent a lot of time at her house.

My grandfather died before I was born.

After momma ran off with Uncle James my granny was so upset it seemed to just drain the life right out her, she took to her room and wouldn't speak to anyone but me, one day she told me it was her fault my momma ran off with uncle James, I never understood that I just figured she was just grieving and blaming herself

Granny died when I was twelve, daddy said she grieved herself to dead and it was my momma's fault and I believed him.

Granny loved my mother; she was her only child, some times when I spend the night at her house I would hear my granny crying."

She held the picture very close as if she was remembering.

"So when I came here to live I had Mr. Reed sell all of my things I didn't have any used for them here, but I did keep a few of momma and my daddy's things.

If you could hand me that little trunk right over there" Mary said pointing to a trunk sitting beside the dresser.

I got the trunk and sit it on a table that was by her chair.

She opened it and started to sit things on the table, one thing I noticed was a bottle of perfume, and I picked it up.

"Was this your mother's?" "Yes, and that has a story of its own.

My Uncle gave her that perfume and when my father found out, he told her to throw it away, she was to never use it, I couldn't understand that until she ran away with him, but Momma didn't throw it away instead she hid it from my father, and sometimes I would catch her holding this bottle and smelling the sweet savor."

"Do you mind if I smell it?" I asked Mary.

"No go ahead."

"For some reason I wasn't shocked when the smell had a hint of baby powder.

"I placed the bottle back on the table and listened as Mary told the story of the things she took out of the truck.

"Mary what was your Mother's name?"

"Her name was Olivia Marie."

"Mary, the furniture that belonged to your mother is in my shop and one day I was cleaning it, I took all the drawers out of the vanity and behind the drawer was a secret compartment and inside was your mother's diary."

I took it out of my bag and placed it in her hands.

Tears welled up in her eyes. "Oh my goodness, this is the greatest thing in the world not even a millions dollars could be a better gift

I thank you from the bottom of my heart." She reached out and took my hand, so you wasn't just interested in the pieces of furniture you have, but you were interested in my mother," she started to cry.

"Mary I read her diary, and I hope after you read it, it will help you to understand things you may have had questions about.

I'm so very happy I got to meet you Mary, I kneel and gave her a hug.

I picked up my bag and started to the door.

"Thank you Ally, you have no idea what you gave me today.

As I walked down the sidewall to the car, I had such a good feeling about what took place today and I was happy that I listened to my dreams and delivered her book of thoughts to her daughter.

Chapter Twenty Two

So do you think now you will be able to put all of this behind you?"

"Yes I really do, Olivia's diary was put into her daughter's hands like she wanted me to do, I haven't had a dream in a while so I think it's over, I just want to get our house done now.

"Thank you Jase, for helping me with all of this drama from a ghost."

As soon as we got home Jase and the guys started working on the house, Jase wanted to get the downstairs done first, so we decided to stay at the B&B until it was finished.

I spend o lot of time packing up the house I was thankful my father was a simple man and didn't have a lot of things.

He just had the necessaries, so it didn't take long to have everything in boxes and stacked out of their way.

"The room off of the kitchen has to be empty because that room is coming down to make more room for the kitchen and dining room." Jase told me.

"Okay, the only things in that room is some boxes my father put in there, I will start there next."

While the guys were carrying out the furniture to take to the shop I took the boxes out of the room, I cried as I packed my dad's clothes that were hanging in the room.

"I miss you daddy so much."

I went thought a few boxes of papers that belonged to my dad.

It looked like he kept everything that was not of importance so I started tossing them away, I came across an envelope that had my dad's handwriting on it, it read. My Love Sofia

Inside the envelope was a picture of my dad and a woman I had never seen before.

The picture looked like it had been taken at someone's house; there were people in the background. My dad looked so young and happy.

As I looked closer at the picture, someone in the background made me gasp, it was Mary, she was younger, but I recognized her, I had never been so confused in my life, who was this woman with my father and how did he know Mary?"

Jase was in the kitchen taking cabinets down.

I took the picture in to show him.

As he looked at the picture he asked me if I was sure it was Mary.

"Yes I'm a hundred percent positive this is Olivia's Daughter the woman I went to see, it's her Jase."

'Okay, I believe you, we will go back and show her this picture and you can find out from her, did you look though the rest of your father's papers maybe there is more pictures."

"No I didn't but I'm going to right now."

"I will help you," He said.

Jase and I spent two hours going through every box and then I searched the house for any more boxes, but we found nothing.

He wrote my Love Sofia, so he was in love with her.

I hoped Mary had the answers to my questions.

When Jase seen I couldn't stop thinking about the picture and wondering about who the woman could be.

He decided the sooner we went and talked to Mary the better and I agreed.

So we left for Georgia we left early because it was a eight hour drive, I was glad I had Lee to take care of the shop while we were away.

We got our room; it was too late to visit Mary today so we had to wait until the next morning.

As I walked down the sidewall again, I hoped she remembered me still.

"Hi may I help you?" the lady at the desk asked.

"I'm here to see Mary Wilkins."

"Oh good, do you know which room is hers?"

"Yes I do, after giving her my name, she wrote it in her book then gave me a name tag.

When I walked into Mary's room she was watching television.

Chapter twenty Three

H*I Mary, do you remember me?"*

"I may be old but I still have my memory" she said "and I will never forget you Ally."

"How are you doing?" I asked her "As well as expected for a ninety four year old. She said with a little laugh...

"Mary while going through some of my father's things I came across a picture and I was hoping you could tell me who the lady in the picture was."

"How should I know that?" she said.

"Because you are also in the picture" I handed her the picture.

She looked at it and then she looked at me.

"Is John Mitchell, your father?" "Yes he is."

The beautiful lady with John is my granddaughter Sofia, she was indeed a beauty.

"Mary can you tell me how they knew each other.

Was it before my mother?

I know you have questions and I will try to help you answer them.

"When Sofia was five years old, her father was killed when one night he jumped a train as the men back them sometimes did, but one night he fell on the track, my daughter was devastated, her and Sofia moved in with me.

John's family had lived next door to me for years; I knew your grandparents, very sweet people.

John and my Sofia grew up together   they were smitten with each other even when they were young.

Then your dad went into the service,   for a year they wrote each other daily.

But then a widow along with his small son moved into the house on our block and Sofia started to babysit his son for him.

And before anyone even realized it Sofia had fallen in love with him and they were married.

When your father came home from the service he was very hurt, but it didn't take him long to meet and marry your mother.

They brought a home not far from his Parents home.

"Was it On Pike Street? I asked.

"Yes, do you remember the place?"

"I grew up in that house." "Oh right" "she said.

Your mother was a great girl and they both were so happy when you were born.

When my father passed away my daughter and I moved back into the house I had grew up in right here in Columbus, and I gave Sofia my house.

Sofia and her husband were happy for a while.

But One day Harold just told her that he felt trapped.

He wanted out of the marriage so he took his son and left town. Sofia was so hurt.

When your mother became ill, your dad never left her side he suffered greatly when she passed away, you were about two years old, when he and Sofia started seeing each other again, she loved your father, and she loved you.

You father suffered great lost in his life, they never married because there wasn't enough time for them.

My beautiful Sofia lost her life when she fell down a flight of stairs and hit her head.

John swore that his daughter would be the only person he would ever love again, when I had my estate sale to move here, your father came to see me and that must have been when he brought the furniture that is now in your store.

I was so sorry to hear of his passing, he was a great man."

"Ally, honey is there anything else I can tell you?"

"Yes what was the address that Sofia lived when she passed?

"My Poppa owned that house is was on Park St.

She reached into the drawer by her bed for a pen and paper and wrote down the address for me when I looked at it I wasn't surprise to see she had written down my address, it all made sense to me now.

That is the reason my Dad had always wanted the big Victorian house, I remember he told me he had always wanted the house, he just didn't tell me why.

But now I know it was because it was Sofia's house.

"Mary, can I ask you another question,

Did you ever live in this house?"

"No not that house, I lived across from it,

My poppa owned houses, he and my mother lived in one when she was carrying me but not for long, my Poppa said.

"Did your granddaughter ever mention to you about having dreams?"

"It's funny; you ask that, she told me one day, her grandmother had visited her in her sleep.

"Mary, thank you so much, I understand things better now."

I gave her a hug goodbye, promising I would keep in touch.

I told Jase everything she told me.

"So are you telling me that Olivia could possibly? Be the girl in your dreams?"

"That is what I have been trying to tell you, but this proves it.

"So that means that Olivia has lived in our house?" he said.

"Oh, my goodness I never thought about that."

"Well didn't you say, Mary, told you her Dad owned the house?

"Yes but she said she had only lived for a little while and accounting to Olivia's diary she hated it there and it was only a short time."

I was ready to go home and get our house done and to stop thinking about the past, I was certain I wouldn't have any more dreams, there was no need for them, I felt like Olivia wanted her daughter to know that she hadn't abandoned her.

Chapter Twenty Four

After only five weeks the downstairs was finally done and I was so happy when our modern future arrived, before the week was over I had everything in place from the pictures on the walls to the accent rugs on my new hardwood floors, I loved my new house, Jase, and his crew did an excellent job on the renovation of our house, it was beautiful.

The outside of the house looked like an up to date beautiful Victorian house and I loved the new land scraping, it was really starting to feel like home.

Now they were starting on the upstairs where there were five very small rooms and a long unnecessary hallway.

Jase was going to tear out the hallway and open up the rooms to make them bigger instead of five rooms there would only be three bedrooms at the end of the hall he was putting in a big bathroom.

I enjoyed staying at the B&B getting to know my sister n law. But it was nice to be back in my house. We stayed in the finished bedroom downstairs.

The new furniture looked really good.

The house looked nothing like it did, when my Father first moved in.

I hope he would have been happy with the new look.

We at last had everything out of the rooms upstairs and the guys had started tearing out walls.

Once the rooms were finished Jase said he was putting in a new up to date staircase.

Then our house would be finished. I was at the shop when Jase called me, he told me to come home.

"Jase, what is wrong?" I could tell something wasn't right in his voice.

"Just come home now, I will talk to you when you get here.

"Martha I need to go home for a little while, but Lee will be here shorty."

"Okay, that's fine we are not too busy this morning.

I could not image why he wanted me home, I really hoped it wasn't to ask my opinion on something, but I also hope no one got hurt.

When I pulled in my driveway my heart sank, there were two police cars and a coroner there.

I jumped out of my car and ran to the door; Jase met me before I could go inside.

"Jase, what is going on, I was almost in tears.

"Ally, calm down no one has been hurt."

"Then why is there a coroner in our driveway?"

I demanded to know.

"Ally, when we tore down some walls, we discovered two skeletons wrapped in plastic inside the wall.

"What? I don't understand." Ally, we found two bodies in the walls upstairs"

"Who were they? We don't know, but the coroner said they have been here for many years, they were wrapped in plastic, it was a man and a woman"

"Oh my god, Jase I know who they are." I started to cry.

"Ally, I know what you are thinking, but we don't know that."

"I do know that, I insisted.

"Ally, I need you to calm down, you can't let this upset you.

"You don't understand Jase. I'm not upset, I'm glad you found Olivia, now she can be put to rest."

They carried the body bags down. I cried because I knew Matthew had killed two innocent people and had gotten away with it, I cried for a little girl that had to grow up thinking her mother deserted her.

Then I thought of Mary, we had to tell her that her mother had been found, and let her give her mother and uncle a proper burial and I would help her.

Jase insisted we stay a few days at the B&B again until the upstairs was completely done, he said he didn't want me back upstairs until then.

And the truth was I didn't want to go back up there and see where they found them, but when I asked Jase he said at the end of the hall.

The next day we went down to the police station and told them everything we knew and I also told them my suspicions on who I thought it was. to me it wasn't suspicions but I didn't think they would take my dreams into considerations so I didn't mention them, I just told them about what Mary told me, after we left the police station, we drove the eight hours to see Mary.

This time Jase went in with me.

When I walked up to the desk, the same woman was there, she looked at me kind of strange.

"Hi we are here to see Mary Wilkins."

"Are you related to Mary?" "No just an old family friend."

"I'm sorry Mary passed away in her sleep on Monday, but she did leave this, she took an envelope out of her desk.

"You are Ally?" "Yes I am" she handed it to me, I thanked her and we walked out I was so sad Jase put his arm around me.

"Jase, Mary passed away Monday on the same day, you found her mother's body."

I opened the envelope inside was a picture I just stared at it, I couldn't believe my eyes.

"Ally who is she? He said when he looked at the picture and seen my reaction.

"It's the girl in my dreams, it is Olivia.

He took the picture out of my hand and turned it over on the back it said Olivia.

I opened the letter and began to read it.

"Dear Ally this is the only picture I have of my mother, my granny gave it to me just before she died, I never showed it to my Poppa.

I want to thank you for going to the trouble to pass on a message to me from my mother, I know now Momma didn't leave me by her choice, she did love me and I can rest now, because this has brought me great comfort, and I hope when you have your daughter, you will know there is nothing or no one that can break the bond between a mother and a daughter, you had that with your mother, you just don't remember, but I do.

You was chosen to deliver a message and to give rest and you have did that, your job is done, so don't go through life thinking you could have did more, because you did do more.

More than you will ever know." Mary

"What makes her think we are having a baby?

Much less having a girl?"

"I don't know, I said as I wiped away the tears.

I wanted to wait to tell you this, because I wanted it to be a surprise but I am pregnant, and I have never told anyone.

I was waiting for the right time to surprise you, I just found out a few days ago.

"Wow I'm surprised" he laughed. "Are you happy?" I asked.

"Yes I'm very happy. We're going to have a baby."

"Wait until my mother hears that she is going to be a grandmother, she will be so happy."

Chapter twenty Five

I don't know think they ever determined that the two bodies that were found were James and Olivia.

But I knew, and now they are at rest beside Mary.

I never had another dream.

Jase and I hang out a lot with Ann and Tony; the guys really hit it off just like I hoped they would.

Jase's, family were so happy about the baby and my ultrasound did reveal we were having a girl, but deep down I kind of already knew that.

Jase refused to let me go upstairs until it was completely finished. And When I did, I was totally shocked. It didn't even resemble the same upstairs, it was very pretty, and the long hallway was gone.

I was very happy with the results.

Once we found out we were having a girl,

Ann helped me decorate her room.

I missed reading about Olivia, and I often wondered what happened.

I guess I would never know. I just felt a connection between Olivia and her family.

I wondered if anyone who had lived in this house,

Before my father move here, if maybe they had the same dreams that I have had?'

After supper, I brought this idea come to Jase.

"I was thinking if I could find out who lived here before my father moved in to this house, maybe they could tell me something about the house and if they had the same dreams?"

"Ally, I thought you said you were going to put this all behind you."

"I know, I want to, I just can't seem to forget Olivia.

"Honey, Olivia is at rest beside her daughter, don't you think you should give it a rest also we have a baby coming, two business to run, our lives are full

And the dreams have stopped, so can you please put it behind you now, I don't want to see you upset over this anymore."

"Yes you are right, I'm sorry, I'm letting it go as of right now."

At Mary request her body was send here to be laid beside her daughter and Granddaughter and now her mother is laid beside her and beside her mother, her uncle is laid.

As I sat in the rocker feeding Olivia her bottle, I look at the picture that sat on the fireplace mantle of my father and Mother and I couldn't help but smile and remember the words he spoke to me.

"One day ally you will raise your family in this house.

I know that is what my father wanted but I knew he would understand that even though the house had been fixed up and updated, this house could never feel like home to me, there was just too much history in it and I still have never felt comfortable here so when Carla announced that her and Joe were getting married and they were moving away. Jase and I decided to put the house up for sale and move into the house beside the B&B so I could run the inn while he ran the antique shop and I loved that idea I was looking forward to moving into the very modern and luxurious Sandcastle B&B.

Lee would run the shop when Jase had to work somewhere else, so everything worked out good.

I kept my promise to my father and I didn't have to do the two things that I have never wanted to do.

Run the shop and live in the big Victorian house.

I have a terrific husband, a beautiful daughter, and my best friend lived two miles from me.

Life was good.

About the author

Brenda lives in Michigan with her husband Duane and her two small mixed Jack Russell dogs, Zoey & Calie,
She likes to read and spend time with her family
They have four children, ten grandchildren, and four great grandchildren.
Brenda loves to write fiction books.
She has written
The Series of "the Damage of Deception"
"The Damage of Deception" Book One
"Empty Vows" Book two
"An Unknown love" Book three
"A Promise Broken" Book four.

Made in the USA
Monee, IL
13 January 2020

20265094R00134